CURIOSITIES OF THE ELDRITCH

THE FIRST GLIMPSE

K.W. BUSSARD

Book Cover by: Joze Groselj 'Vitogh'

Sigil Design by: Dzmitry Zasimovich

Map by Corin Raldekaln

1st edition 2025

CONTENTS

THE SHOPKEEPER

INTRODUCTION

Hidden in the twisting streets of Arden's Wake, there is an alleyway that only appears when it is meant to. Revealing a place of forgotten relics, forbidden texts, the strange and mysterious. It exists in a very peculiar state. It is neither fully in this world nor entirely out of it. Hanging above the door is an old, weathered, wooden sign with faded golden letters catching the light of a nearby lantern: Curiosities. It is a simple name, perhaps, but the customers who venture inside quickly learn that simplicity is not what it seems.

I am the keeper of this shop and the narrator of its tales. You may call me Aldwyn. I have gone by many names across limitless timelines and realities, though this one has stuck the longest...for now. I am old enough to have forgotten how many winters I have seen, though my bones remind me more often than I would like. My long, white beard is long enough to tuck into my belt. Which, regrettably, I have done more than once by accident. I often lose my glasses and my memory is not what it used to be. Sometimes, I catch myself in mid-thought and have to retrace my steps. Still, the shop and I get along well enough. We have been tied together for longer than I care to recall.

You see, each and every item in this shop carries a story. They tell not just about the past but also about potential destiny. These objects also do not simply wait to be purchased by just anyone... they choose their owners. A cracked mirror that reveals truths long buried. A music box that plays the song of your soul's deepest yearning. An inkwell rumored to give life to whatever is written in its ink, though at a cost most find too steep. Some offer salvation. Others bring ruin.

It is not my place to judge the choices people make. But instead, I can guide you through the interpretation...or at least try to. That is... if my memory does not fail me. I am a reluctant caretaker of fates, offering the keys to futures that only my customers can unlock. And yet, even though I may be a grumpy old man, I have grown fond of the travelers who step through these doors. Their triumphs. Their failures. Even the echoes of their choices linger long after they have gone, written into the tomes that line the shelves of the Athenaeum. Oh, yes... That is the library this shop is bound to. It holds what feeds my quaint little shop. It exists outside of our reality and time. In the void, you could say. Containing all knowledge across the infinite of time and space and from all possible realities.

On this particular night within the shop, the shelves groaned a bit more than usual beneath the weight of the old tomes and various other trinkets that quietly vibrated with anticipation. The stale air carried its usual blend of scents: sandalwood, candle wax, dust, and... is that garlic?. ..and asparagus? Those gargoyles outside the door must be snacking again. It always gives them the worst gas that just seeps through the door cracks.

The bell above the door jingled suddenly, announcing a visitor.

In walked a young man. The door shut behind him. His presence was causing a stir and rattle within the shelves, as if everything was whispering about the new arrival. His eyes darted around, uncertain as to what this place is exactly or how he happened across it. The young man was dressed plainly enough. His coat was mended with careful stitches. His boots looked worn from long travels on the road. There was a wonder in his gaze. The kind that belonged to someone searching for something they could not yet name.

"Ah! A customer...Welcome! Come in, come in," I said. "What is it you seek?"

He hesitated to respond for a moment, still looking about the room.

"I...I don't know?" He fumbled with his words. "Not even sure what 'here' is?"

"Few ever do," I replied as I scratched at my beard. "But the shop knows. It always knows."

The young man walked around for a bit, looking at this and that. Most folks do wander around. As he approached, a faint glow started to emanate from a shelf to his left. He looked over at the object. It was a small box made of dark wood, etched with intricate patterns. Although they were worn to the point it was almost too faint to see. He reached for it, his hand trembling ever so slightly.

"That," I muttered, squinting at the object to make sure I remembered right, "is the Lamenter's box. It is said to hold the final words of those who never had the chance to speak them. Or... was it the box that hums lullabies? No, no, it is definitely the first one."

He turned it over in his hands, his expression unreadable. "What's the cost?"

"Not all costs are measured in currency, my boy. Some are paid in ways you cannot yet foresee."

He stood there for a moment, weighing my words. Then, with a resolute nod, he placed the box on the counter. "I'll take it."

As I wrapped the box in soft velvet and handed it to him, I could not help but wonder what path he had set himself upon. Would this item bring him closure? Or would it open wounds he wasn't prepared to face? That was not for me to decide. My role was merely to watch, facilitate, and grumble when the dust on the shelves got the better of me.

As quickly as he had arrived, he was gone. The door closed behind him, sounding another ring from the bell. The shop fell silent again, save for the faint crackle of a candle burning low. "Where did I place my ledger this time?" I mumbled out loud. "Ah, yes! Here it is," while I moved some scattered newspapers to jot down the latest transaction.

Another story begins. Another thread added to the tapestry of fate. Such is what happens in the Curiosities shop. Each visitor, each relic weaves a singular and connected tale. The stories will continue for me to tell their tale to you. The individuals that find their way to my shop, their thoughts, and trials... All are endlessly fascinating, and I do enjoy being nosey. Some are stories of history retold, while others are ever unpredictable because their outcome depends on the customer. Perhaps, one day, you will find yourself here, too. When you do, be sure to listen carefully. The items have much to say, and their whispers are not easily ignored.

VOLUME 1

The First Glimpse

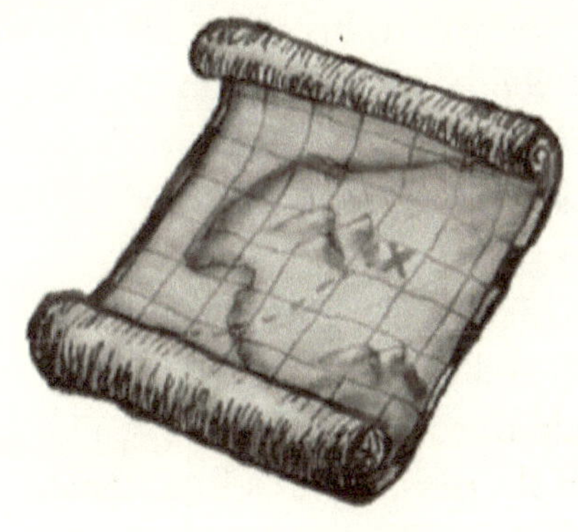

Chapter One

CORIN'S TALE

Corin Raldekaln jolted awake in a cold sweat. His broad chest rose and fell with ragged breaths beneath the scratchy wool blanket. Beads of sweat clung stubbornly to his brow. He rubbed at his eyes as he tried to banish the echoes of his nightmare... the rush of water... an outstretched hand... the silence that followed.

Years had passed since Marek drowned in that river, and yet the nightmares never ceased.

Corin pushed himself upright, exhaling in exhaustion. His stout, dwarven frame shifted the creaky wooden cot beneath him. The small, dim room was faintly accented by morning sunlight squeezing through gaps in the wooden shutters. It was a functionally modest space for a traveler rather than a permanent resident. Comfort was not a luxury this room provided in spades, other than a place to sleep. Against the far wall, a narrow table sat cluttered with half-finished maps and pencil nubs. Spilled ink stained the table's surface. A trunk sat at the end of the bed, clothes lousily tossed inside, half hanging out.

Corin ran a calloused hand through his dark, unkempt hair before rubbing thoughtfully at his beard. His fingers brushed lightly across the silver beads woven into its thick braids. Most dwarfs earned beads through feats of accomplishment or adornment from their houses. This was a dwarven tradition he refused to abandon.

This wasn't the life he'd imagined for himself.

He had once dreamed of mapping every unseen corner of the world. His dream to become a renowned master cartographer, whose work would be remembered for ages. He had trained meticulously to hone his skills over his long lifetime. But after Marek...

Corin scoffed at himself. Marek was more than a companion. He was a brother. Their bond was forged through adventure, and the trust between them could move mountains. They had journeyed countless rivers, scaled mountains and explored forgotten ruins all across the world. Mutual hunger for discovery drove them on further.

The river that day had been stronger than either of them had anticipated. The currents were deceptively fierce and the rocks dangerously sharp. He could still feel the icy chill of water splashing against his boots, the raw helplessness as Marek slipped beneath the surface.

Corin's hands clenched in frustration. He had spent years buried in the ink and parchment of his work, attempting to forget. But no map could chart a way forward when the weight of the past refused to release its grip.

He sighed deeply as he pushed himself off the cot, stretching stiffness from weary limbs. His boots beside the bed, he slipped them on, securing the straps. His satchel rested near the door.

Arden's Wake had become his refuge. A city vast enough to lose himself within. He had convinced himself he remained here for work. The truth was more straightforward than that. It was easier to hide in one place, to walk familiar streets, and pretend he was content with the routine, than it was to face his fears out charting the unknown frontier.

Restlessness tugged at his thoughts today.

"Perhaps a walk through the streets would clear my mind," he said to himself.

Corin slung the satchel over his shoulder and stepped toward the door.

He pulled the door closed behind him. The lock clicked into place with a familiar thunk. He paused for a moment and rested his hand lightly on the worn wooden surface. It was strange how even a temporary space could become a refuge.

He turned toward the stairs, and the old wooden floor creaked gently beneath his heavy boots. Morning had fully arrived at the inn. Murmurs of conversation drifted upward, punctuated occasionally by laughter or the scrape of a chair. The scent of cooked meats and baked goods mingled enticingly, though Corin felt little hunger.

Descending the stairs, he glanced around the warmly lit common room. A scattering of patrons filled the tables, some lingered from the night before, others just beginning their day. Behind the counter stood Garret, the burly innkeeper whose hearty manner was a staple of the establishment. He caught sight of Corin and offered a welcoming nod, wiping his hands on a cloth before stepping forward.

"Morning, Corin. Rest well?"

"Well enough, thank you."

He reached beneath the counter and produced a plate with a chunk of stale bread and a small cup of juice, placing them onto the polished wood.

"It ain't much, but it'll get you started. Baker hasn't come by yet."

Corin accepted the offering gratefully, nodding his thanks.

"It'll do just fine."

He chewed absently on the coarse bread, washing it down with a few gulps of juice. Neither flavor nor texture registered with him; food had become more a necessity than a comfort. After a brief moment, he placed the empty cup back onto the counter and slid a few coins toward Garret, who swiftly pocketed them with a nod.

"Heading out early today?" Garret asked casually, already turning to serve another patron.

Corin shrugged, adjusting the satchel at his side. "Just need to clear my head."

Garret nodded again, understanding evident in his eyes. "Stay safe out there, then."

Corin gave a faint, acknowledging smile before heading toward the inn's entrance. He pushed open the heavy wooden door and stepped outside into the streets of Arden's Wake, letting the fresh air wash away the closeness of the inn, if not the lingering shadows within his mind.

Corin stepped out into the narrow streets of Arden's Wake, breathing in the familiar scents of morning: damp stone, woodsmoke from early cookfires, and the distant aroma of fresh bread baking somewhere nearby.

The comforting noises of the city waking surrounded him, gently masking the lingering unease from his restless night.

As he began his walk, Corin fell into a well-worn rhythm. His boots moved almost automatically along cobblestone roads he had walked countless times before. Merchants began arranging their wares, calling greetings to one another as shop doors swung open, spilling warm light into the street. Carts clattered by, wheels splashing through small puddles left from overnight rains. Despite the vibrancy of life surrounding him, Corin felt strangely detached, as though he walked through a city he no longer fully inhabited.

He passed by familiar landmarks: the blacksmith's forge, alive with sparks; the small bakery whose owner always smiled kindly, even though Corin rarely stopped to buy anything; and the market square already humming with early-morning trade. He knew every alleyway, every corner of Arden's Wake, having mapped them himself over countless days spent pacing its streets, hoping to regain the purpose he'd lost along the way.

Corin's mind drifted, his steps slowing as memories intruded. His thoughts returned to Marek, as they always seemed to, pulling him back to another time, another place. Arden's Wake faded around him, replaced by jagged mountain peaks, lush valleys, and wide-open skies. For a brief moment, he remembered what it felt like to stand on the brink of discovery, to sketch lines on parchment that represented places no one had ever seen. The thrill of exploration, the satisfaction of new paths charted. He had lived for those moments. Until that river took it all away.

His jaw tightened. The maps he now drew were merely shadows of the ones he'd once crafted. Instead of new lands, he now filled pages with repetitive streets and familiar paths, as though repeating lines on paper could somehow quiet the memories whispering at the edges of his mind.

While lost in thought, Corin paused mid-step. He squinted down the familiar street, confusion etched deeply into his features. Every building, storefront, and cobblestone of Arden's Wake had long since been committed to memory. Yet today, something was unmistakably out of place.

Between two weathered buildings, a narrow alleyway stretched back into shadows, framed by faded brickwork and moss-covered stone. Corin frowned, his dark brows knitting together. He could have sworn he'd mapped every inch of this district. Had this alleyway always been here?

Curiosity sparked within him, quietly pushing aside lingering thoughts of Marek and his past. With cautious steps, Corin approached the mouth of the alley. It felt strangely isolated from the bustle of morning life. A pocket of silence amidst the city's daily noise.

What is this?

He hesitated, glancing briefly back at the bustling life of the street behind him. Then, curiosity getting the better of him, Corin moved toward the newly discovered alleyway.

Corin

How odd.

Halfway down the alley, his eyes caught sight of a dim, flickering glow from a small lantern illuminating the doorway of what appeared to be a forgotten shop. A wooden sign hung above the entrance, weathered and faded with age. Corin strained to make out the inscription.

"Curiosities," he read aloud, the word barely a whisper.

The name intrigued him, calling up memories of adventure, the thrill of discovering something unknown. Corin moved forward slowly, noticing two small stone gargoyles perched above the doorway, their lifeless eyes staring down, eternally watchful. He studied them briefly, a faint smile tugging at his lips.

"Charming guardians for a shop like this." he mocked.

As he drew nearer, the neglect of the shop became clear. Layers of dust covered the worn wooden frame, and spiderwebs stretched lazily from corner to corner. Yet something about this forgotten storefront spoke to him, whispering quietly beneath the silence. It resonated within him, a reflection of his own hidden existence in Arden's Wake.

His hand reached instinctively toward the tarnished brass door handle, hesitation briefly crossing his mind. Was this curiosity or foolishness? But before doubt could fully take hold, the door opened with a soft creak, accompanied by the gentle chime of a bell overhead.

Corin stood motionless at the threshold, uncertainty holding him in place. Before he could reconsider, an odd, pungent gust of wind pushed lightly at his back, urging him forward.

The door shut softly behind Corin, muffling the familiar noises of Arden's Wake until they were only a distant memory. I smiled from behind the counter, shuffling papers aimlessly before suddenly realizing a visitor had entered. Visitors? Goodness me, I hadn't heard the bell. Had it rung? Well, it must have.

"Ah! A customer! Yes, yes, welcome indeed!" I exclaimed warmly, adjusting my spectacles. "I was just...organizing. Or rather, planning to organize. Oh, never mind all that. Welcome to my humble Curiosities shop!"

Corin stood motionless near the doorway, allowing his eyes to adjust to the shop's dim, amber glow. A peculiar warmth filled the interior, mingled with the scents of aged parchment, spices, and something oddly pungent. Oh yes, that smell... distinctive, unmistakable.

I caught his wrinkled nose and chuckled softly, shaking my head in apology. "The gargoyles," I explained with a conspiratorial whisper, nodding toward the door. "They argue constantly, and when they get excited... well, let's just say the air takes on a certain, shall we call it, fragrance."

As if on cue, muffled, grumbling voices drifted faintly through the closed door.

"It was your fault, you stone-brained lump! If you'd stop passing gas..."

"Oh, always blaming me! If you'd stop babbling nonsense... you know I have a nervous disposition."

Corin glanced back at the door, startled, before returning his cautious gaze to the shop interior.

"Don't mind them," I added cheerfully. "They've been at it for decades. Or centuries, perhaps... I can never quite remember."

The interior stretched impossibly deeper than its modest exterior would suggest. Shelves and tables cluttered together, overflowing with peculiar artifacts: dusty books, intricate statuettes, shimmering baubles, and curious objects that defied immediate identification. Each seemed to await someone specific, patiently biding their time.

Toward the back of the shop, something metallic crashed loudly to the floor, followed by a tiny, exasperated squeak.

"Ah," I sighed fondly, "that's Fizzlewick, our gnome caretaker. He's, uh... enthusiastic, if somewhat prone to accidents."

"I'm fine!" came a muffled squeak from the shadows, followed by the sound of frantic sweeping and clinking glassware.

Corin slowly stepped forward, boots creaking on worn wooden floorboards. He reached instinctively toward a small brass astrolabe on a nearby shelf, but quickly withdrew his hand, hesitating as though he feared disturbing the fragile quiet of the place.

"Oh, don't worry about touching things," I assured him kindly. "The objects here often choose visitors, rather than the other way around. Do mind the sharp ones... sometimes they bite."

Corin's brow furrowed at that, understandably confused. I smiled warmly, feeling slightly forgetful again. "I mean... well, not literally, usually. Anyway, please, look around. Something is sure to find you soon enough."

Indeed, as if responding to my words, Corin's eyes drifted toward a small pile of forgotten odds and ends atop an antique cabinet. There, glimmering faintly beneath a veil of dust, rested a slender bookmark, etched delicately with faint, shifting runes. He stepped closer, drawn irresistibly toward it.

"What... what is this?" Corin asked quietly, lifting the bookmark with delicate reverence.

"Oh, that," I replied brightly, eyes lighting with recognition. "A lending card of sorts. Grants entry to a fragment of the Athenaeum. A library of infinite knowledge that exists beyond space, time, and realities... beyond infinite questions, and yes, infinite challenge."

"Infinite challenge?"

"Well, of course," I said, waving a hand vaguely. "Every visitor's experience is unique, you see. Some find answers, others uncover more questions. A rare few, if they are brave enough, or foolish enough, might even discover themselves."

A distant clang echoed through the shop again, followed by another squeak from Fizzlewick. "Nothing broken this time, I swear!"

I chuckled, shaking my head. "You see? The Athenaeum isn't so different from this shop. It's beautiful, chaotic, and full of surprises. But you must choose to enter of your own free will, no one else's."

Corin hesitated, staring intently at the bookmark. A mixture of fear, curiosity, and quiet desperation played across his features, stirring sympathy in my heart. It was a look I'd seen before. One I knew all too well.

At last, Corin's expression hardened with determination, his voice scarcely above a whisper. "Yes. I choose to try."

"Excellent!" I exclaimed, clapping my hands once, delighted. "A fine choice! Or at least, an interesting one. Those are often the best."

As he clasped the bookmark in his hand, its runes flared gently, bathing his palm in soft warmth. I smiled warmly, gesturing toward the shadows beyond the shelves.

"Then step forward, Corin Raldekaln. Your journey begins now. Let's see what awaits you, shall we?"

Behind me came another muffled crash, followed by the exasperated voice of the gnome caretaker: "Everything's still under control!"

I turned slightly, raising an eyebrow. "Do try not to set the shop ablaze this time, Fizzlewick!"

Corin cast a final bewildered glance at me before stepping forward into the waiting unknown. I settled back against the counter, watching him vanish into the shadows, and smiled to myself.

"Good luck, my young friend," I murmured softly. "You're certainly going to need it."

The moment Corin's fingers closed fully around the bookmark, warmth surged from his palm, coursing through him like liquid fire. He gasped, eyes widening as the world around him shifted abruptly. Shelves blurred and walls melted away into nothingness, dissolving into a swirl of indistinct shapes and colors. For an instant, he felt suspended between realities, untethered and weightless.

Just as quickly, the disorienting sensation ceased. His boots pressed firmly onto solid ground once more. Blinking away the lingering dizziness, Corin took in his new surroundings.

He stood now in a sprawling chamber illuminated by a soft, golden glow. Towering bookshelves lined every visible wall, stretching upward into shadows that concealed their true height. Countless books and scrolls occupied every available inch, their spines and covers adorned with titles that shifted gently when observed directly, as if reluctant to fully reveal themselves.

A reading nook stretched before Corin, bathed in a warm, golden glow that pulsed faintly with its own gentle rhythm, almost like a heartbeat. It felt alive, the air thick with presence. Shelves climbed upward, towering impossibly high, their upper reaches dissolving not merely into shadow, but into something beyond perception, as though reality itself grew thin near the ceiling. Corin strained his eyes upward, feeling suddenly small beneath the weight of infinity.

Books filled every available space, meticulously arranged yet somehow chaotic. Some volumes were pristine, bound in bright leather or softly glowing cloth, while others lay cracked and weathered, their spines faded and peeling. Their titles shimmered and shifted as he tried to read them, each word dancing just beyond clarity, teasing him with secrets he was not yet ready to know.

The air carried a rich fragrance, both comforting and strangely unsettling. The scent of ancient parchment and ink blended softly with a subtle floral note of lavender, perhaps but beneath this gentle fragrance lurked an edge, sharp and metallic, like the memory of distant storms. Corin inhaled slowly, his chest tightening in response, his heartbeat quickening in sudden apprehension.

Silence enveloped the room, but this was not the oppressive stillness of emptiness. Instead, it felt charged, vibrant with an invisible energy. He could almost sense the room breathing gently around him, as if waiting patiently for something or someone.

He stepped forward cautiously, boots sinking slightly into a plush rug that stretched along the length of the corridor. Looking down, he saw threads intricately woven together, strands of shadow interlaced seamlessly with shimmering light, shifting subtly beneath his weight. A strange sensation surged up through his feet, electric and alive, sending a shiver down his spine. Corin instinctively recoiled, his breath catching sharply.

"What... is this place?" he whispered, the words slipping out involuntarily. They sounded distant, distorted, as though they'd been plucked directly from his mind rather than spoken aloud.

An answer came immediately. The voice was immense, omnipresent, neither masculine nor feminine. It was vast, as boundless as the night sky, resonating with a quiet authority that made Corin feel insignificant, a tiny droplet lost in an endless sea.

"Welcome to your first glimpse of the Athenaeum. Here, you must confront what you carry. Only then may you leave."

The words carved themselves deep into his consciousness, heavy and powerful, pressing upon him like the charged air before a storm breaks.

"What does that mean?" Corin demanded, his voice trembling with fear and anger alike. He spun around, searching for a face, a figure...some tangible source of this intrusion, but saw only shelves, silent and unmoving.

The charged silence returned, broken only by a faint hum that seemed to emanate from within the books themselves. Corin tightened his grip on the bookmark, his knuckles turning pale. It pulsed gently, aligning its rhythm to match the hum. The bookmark felt warm, disturbingly alive in his palm, and he shuddered at the sensation.

He forced himself forward again, leaving the strange reading nook behind as it faded into memory. Ahead, a flicker of light beckoned him deeper into the corridor, like a beacon urging him onward. As he moved forward, the towering shelves closed tighter around him, their heights bending inward oppressively, almost conspiratorially. The whispering grew louder, carrying an undertone of judgment and inquiry.

The rug beneath his boots abruptly transitioned into cold, uneven stone, and Corin nearly stumbled at the sudden change. Each step sent shockwaves reverberating through his body, the sounds of his own footsteps echoing unnaturally, stretching far ahead into the unseen darkness. His throat tightened painfully as anxiety pressed in on him, panic rising within his chest. Every instinct screamed at him to turn back, to flee the suffocating corridor, but Corin knew deep down there was no going back, not now.

He had crossed the threshold. The Athenaeum had already claimed him.

The whispers intensified, cutting through his thoughts with frightening clarity, no longer indistinct murmurs but familiar, accusing voices, each word sharp as a blade, sinking into his mind.

"Do you remember the river?" a voice asked softly, cold and precise, like a dagger wrapped delicately in silk.

Another voice, painfully familiar, echoed immediately after. *"You should have waited."*

Then Marek's voice pierced through. *"My hand was right there, Corin. Why didn't you reach for it?"*

Corin stopped sharply, breath catching, panic surging through his veins. He spun around desperately, searching the shelves for the source, but the whispers had not come from the books. They rose from within him, escaping from a place buried so deeply he'd tried desperately to forget. He clenched his fists, breathing raggedly as guilt tightened its grip around his heart.

"This isn't real," he whispered fiercely, voice trembling. "It's just... just a trick."

Yet the voices ignored his denial, relentless and merciless.

"You carry him still."

"Your maps can't guide you here."

"Do you even know where you're going?"

The final question struck him with physical force. Corin staggered, the weight of it pulling him to a halt. It was true. He didn't know where he was going. Not here, not anywhere. His life had been reduced to meaningless routine, an empty existence devoid of purpose, forever running from the past. The Athenaeum knew this. It was exposing him, stripping away the false comforts he'd carefully built.

The corridor constricted further, shelves pressing inward until he felt utterly trapped. The distant flickering light, once welcoming, now seemed impossibly far away, fading with every passing heartbeat. Forcing himself to move, Corin trudged forward, the stone beneath his feet growing colder, harsher with each step.

As he passed one of the shelves, titles on a small cluster of books suddenly illuminated themselves softly, seizing his attention. His breath caught sharply, the titles too familiar, too personal:

"Corin's Folly: The Expedition That Failed"

"The Cartographer's Doubt: Paths Left Uncharted"

"Marek's River: A Life Lost in the Current"

"No," Corin gasped, tearing his gaze away, stumbling forward blindly. "This isn't fair!"

But the Athenaeum gave no reply. It didn't have to. Its silence was condemnation enough.

Driven now by sheer desperation, Corin pressed forward, eyes fixed firmly on the flickering light. It finally surged to meet him, washing over him in a wave of gentle warmth, swallowing the oppressive corridor and shelves behind him.

For an instant, there was nothing but brilliant whiteness... pure, cleansing, yet terrifying in its emptiness. He floated weightlessly, breathless and suspended, before reality slowly returned around him.

Corin found himself standing in a vast, circular chamber, whose walls rose infinitely into a dim, distant haze. At its center, illuminated by an ethereal glow, stood a solitary pedestal holding a single, blank map.

Approaching cautiously, Corin studied the pristine parchment, its edges slightly frayed, suggesting age yet untouched by ink. His heart thudded painfully within his chest. He reached out hesitantly, fingers trembling as they hovered just above the waiting paper.

The Athenaeum's voice spoke again, gentler now but still impossibly vast.

"This map represents your burden, Corin. It remains blank because you have not yet chosen your path. You must decide whether to remain trapped by guilt or to chart the way forward, no matter how uncertain."

Corin stared down at the empty page, a surge of emotion threatening to overwhelm him. His past was written in regret, but now he was faced with the possibility of writing a new future.

His hand steadied. He drew a deep, determined breath, and touched the pencil tip to the waiting parchment.

"Why show me this?" Corin whispered, his voice a fragile thread breaking the oppressive silence. He stared helplessly at the blank map, frustration mingling with despair. "What am I supposed to do?"

The voice returned, low and steady, filling the chamber without echo yet somehow resonating deep within his chest. ***The map reflects what you carry, Corin. It remains blank because your path has been abandoned. You must choose: will you chart a way forward, or leave it empty?***

Corin's breath caught sharply, his chest tightening painfully. Images flashed vividly through his mind. The unfinished maps left abandoned in frustration, opportunities he'd allowed to pass him by, and then, with painful clarity, Marek's terrified expression as he slipped beneath the river's unforgiving currents. Corin squeezed his eyes shut, desperately willing the memories away, but the Athenaeum's power was relentless. The past would not remain buried here.

As his heart pounded against his ribs, the room shifted subtly around him. Corin opened his eyes, startled, stepping back as three ornate mirrors shimmered into existence around the pedestal. Their silver surfaces rippled gently, almost alive, catching and reflecting the warm, golden light in strange patterns that danced and pulsed hypnotically.

His reflection appeared first in the left mirror, and Corin felt an unexpected ache in his chest. He recognized this version of himself immediately... a young dwarf, full of bright-eyed ambition and unwavering confidence. This younger Corin sketched lines upon parchment with effortless precision, his strong hands steady and sure. There was a fire behind his eyes, the passion of someone who believed he could chart the unknown, someone who still trusted himself without question.

The mirror in the center showed the Corin he had become: older, worn down by sleepless nights and relentless grief. His features were etched deeply with lines of worry, doubt, and regret. His eyes appeared haunted, sunken beneath dark circles, desperately seeking redemption but never quite finding it. The hands that once moved with confidence now trembled visibly, his maps marked with jagged, hesitant strokes, incomplete and abandoned. All testaments to a life frozen by indecision.

Corin's heart grew heavier as his gaze moved slowly to the third mirror. At first, the reflection appeared obscured, hidden behind a haze of uncertainty. He leaned forward cautiously, straining to see clearly. Gradually, the mist lifted, revealing a figure so broken and gaunt that it hardly seemed like him at all. His face was hollow, eyes dull and empty, devoid of any spark. Torn maps lay scattered at his feet, remnants of dreams shattered and forgotten, abandoned forever.

A chill ran through him as he stood frozen before the mirrors, unable to look away. The weight of these reflections pressed heavily upon his heart, each vision more haunting and painful than the last.

The Athenaeum's voice returned softly now, almost gentle, tinged with a note of compassion. ***"Three paths lie before you, Corin: the past, the present, and the future. The past holds wisdom but cannot be changed. The present holds truth but slips quickly from your grasp. The future holds possibility, yet it remains uncertain. You alone must choose."***

Corin's breath grew ragged, each inhale a struggle against the tightening in his chest. His heart and mind warred fiercely within him. The past beckoned with its nostalgic comfort, reminding him of the dwarf he once was, brimming with promise. The present reflected his failures and pain with brutal honesty. But the future terrified him. To see himself reduced to this hollow shadow, utterly lost and broken, was almost unbearable. Yet within that terrible vision, something glimmered faintly... a spark of possibility, fragile and delicate, a whisper of hope amid ruin.

"I can't change the past," Corin whispered, voice shaking with vulnerability and resolve. "And I can't keep living like this."

Slowly, he raised his trembling hand, reaching toward the third mirror, toward the reflection that frightened him most. His palm hovered mere inches from the cool glass, hesitation and fear gripping him tightly. The bookmark in his other hand pulsed with urgency, warmth spreading through his fingers, urging him onward. He swallowed hard, steadied himself, and pressed his palm firmly against the shimmering surface.

The world seemed to hold its breath. Beneath his touch, the mirror trembled, its surface rippling violently like water disturbed by a stone. The broken reflection stared back at him, its hollow eyes locked onto his, daring him to look away. A chill crawled along Corin's spine, but he held firm, refusing to retreat.

The bookmark in his hand flared brightly, its runes blazing fiercely, rearranging themselves faster than his eyes could follow. Its glow intensified, becoming nearly blinding. Corin gritted his teeth against the sudden surge of whispers that erupted in his mind. Voices layered over one another, pressing upon him relentlessly:

"The future waits for no one."
"Each step reshapes your path."
"Do you fear what lies ahead?"

Corin's breathing grew rapid, each breath shaky and desperate. He wanted to shout at the voices, demand they give him peace to think, but he knew they would not relent. This was the Athenaeum's truth laid bare. Not comfort, but clarity. Not reassurance, but revelation. It was a place where illusions fell away, leaving only reality, stark and unforgiving.

"I won't let fear control me anymore," he whispered fiercely, his voice wavering but determined.

The moment the words left his lips, a sound like shattering ice filled the chamber. The mirror beneath his hand fractured violently, cracks spiderwebbing outward in jagged lines of brilliant light. Corin staggered backward, shielding his face as shards burst free, dissolving instantly into swirling fragments of shimmering mist.

The entire chamber began to distort wildly, angles shifting and warping, reality itself losing cohesion. The mirrors melted away, their fragments spiraling upwards and fading into the endless heights above. Corin shielded himself instinctively, heart pounding fiercely, adrenaline surging through him as the room's chaos surged and subsided, leaving him alone once more.

Slowly, silence settled around him, heavy and profound, punctuated only by the quiet rhythm of his ragged breaths. The mirrors had vanished, leaving only the pedestal before him, the map atop it still blank yet somehow charged with purpose. Corin stood for a moment, catching his breath, feeling changed, scarred, yes, but lighter as well, as though he'd taken his first real breath in years.

The voice returned gently, softer now, tinged unmistakably with approval:

"You've made your choice, Corin. Now, you must walk forward and confront what lies ahead."

Corin exhaled deeply, squared his shoulders, and stepped resolutely forward into the unknown.

CHAPTER TWO

THE FIRST CHALLENGE

THE RIVER

Corin stood before the pedestal, the smooth surface of the map empty and lifeless. His pulse quickened as faint threads of pale light flickered beneath the blank surface. At first, they were subtle, delicate lines, like veins waking from sleep but then the illumination grew stronger. The lines twisted and turned, intertwining in patterns that shifted and changed as though alive.

Mesmerized, Corin leaned closer, drawn to the hypnotic movements, trying to decipher meaning within the writhing paths. Yet before understanding could take hold, the ground beneath his feet trembled softly, a subtle warning he nearly missed.

A voice filled the chamber once more, echoing in his ears with commanding certainty:

"Step forward and face what lies ahead."

Corin's heart raced as he glanced around, uncertain, sensing the inevitability of change in the voice's tone. The map glowed brighter still, its movements intensifying until its light swallowed his vision entirely.

Before Corin could react, the chamber began dissolving around him, with a quiet, unsettling inevitability. The walls faded like mist dispersing at dawn, taking shelves lined with ancient books and artifacts with them.

The pedestal, moments before so solid beneath his fingertips, melted away, leaving his hands grasping at empty air.

Corin spun, trying to anchor himself to something tangible, but even the endless ceiling receded upward into darkness. Reality blurred around him, leaving behind only the faint, echoing remnants of the commanding voice.

Then, silence.

When Corin opened his eyes, the familiar chamber had vanished entirely. Instead, he found himself standing alone in a vast, barren landscape that stretched endlessly in every direction. A cold, dry wind whispered harshly, stinging his throat and sharpening his senses.

The sudden emptiness pressed upon him, oppressive and stark. The landscape was cracked and lifeless, a desolate realm he now faced utterly alone.

Corin stepped forward cautiously, his boots crunching against dry, cracked earth. Ahead, stretching endlessly to either side, lay a wide, turbulent river. Its waters were black and restless, churning violently beneath a surface that seemed to boil. The riverbanks appeared wounded, fractured and split as if long deprived of nourishment.

The land around the river was equally harsh. Skeletons of once-grand trees stood twisted and lifeless, their brittle limbs clawing hopelessly toward an empty sky. Silence clung heavily, only broken by the low, guttural roar rising from the chaotic current.

Corin felt his heartbeat quicken again, uncertainty twisting his stomach. As he gazed into the river, he noticed movement beneath its murky surface... dark, writhing shadows coiling within the raging waters. An instinctive dread crept over him; he knew, deep in his bones, that whatever lurked beneath was watching him, waiting.

He tightened his grip around the card still clutched in his palm. It pulsed gently, reassuring yet insistent, urging him forward into the uncertainty of the river's edge.

As Corin now stood at the river's edge, the card in his hand grew warmer, pulsing insistently. The commanding voice returned, softer this time, yet no less resolute.

Corin's breath caught as the card's symbols shifted before his eyes, clearly illustrating his decision:

On one side, he saw the river branching into countless gentle streams, weaving gracefully through the broken land. Everywhere its waters touched, vibrant greenery burst forth, flowers blossomed, and trees sprang up with lush, abundant growth. Life flourished across a landscape reborn, the wounds of the land healed by the river's careful guidance.

Yet, when he turned his gaze to the opposite side, the river surged freely, wild and unchecked. It carved deep, violent canyons into the earth, beautiful yet destructive in its raw power. The surrounding lands remained untouched... stark, harsh, and barren.

Corin stared at both visions, torn between the promise of renewal and the fear of unleashing something darker beneath those roiling waters. The shadows beneath the river twisted, as if sensing his hesitation, reminding him that no choice came without consequence.

Corin knelt at the riverbank, fingers trembling as they brushed the icy, unyielding water. The river tugged at him, cold and relentless, awakening a painful familiarity deep within his chest.

Suddenly, vivid memories surged forward, sharp and overwhelming:

He was standing by another river, years earlier. Marek's voice echoed clearly, cautious but drowned by Corin's own confidence. "We should wait. The current's too strong," Marek had warned, uncertainty etched deeply into his face.

But Corin had ignored the warning, so sure of his own maps, his own judgment. He saw the exact moment Marek's footing failed, felt again the icy water on his own skin, saw his friend's desperate eyes searching for rescue, a rescue that never came.

Guilt tightened around his chest, suffocating and raw. His breath shortened to rapid gasps. The whispers rose from the river, sharp and accusatory:

"Why didn't you listen?"
"You thought you knew better."

"Do you think he forgives you?"

Corin pressed his hands over his ears, but the voices pierced deeper, relentless. "Stop!" he cried out, voice cracking under the weight of unresolved pain. "It wasn't my fault... I didn't..." But his protest died, unfinished. He wasn't even sure he believed his own words.

The whispers subsided, replaced by the calm, firm voice of the Library, cutting through his anguish.

"The river does not forgive, Corin. It moves forward. Will you?"

Corin's breath steadied slowly as he lifted his gaze, staring at the card pulsing in his palm. This was no longer about Marek, nor about past mistakes. It was about the choice now before him, and the courage needed to face it.

Corin rose slowly, boots sinking slightly into the softening earth at the river's edge. The barren landscape stretched out before him, cracked and aching for relief. He felt the weight of choice pressing upon him like never before.

To guide the river's immense power would mean renewal. Life brought forth from emptiness, a chance at redemption. Yet the dark shapes twisting beneath the river's surface warned clearly of hidden dangers. To let it flow unchecked would be safer, but would leave this land broken and lifeless, another path abandoned, another failure marked on his soul.

Corin stared down at the glowing symbols shifting restlessly on the card. His voice came out in a whisper, barely audible even to himself. "Marek would have..." He stopped abruptly. No, this decision wasn't about Marek. It wasn't about the guilt he carried or the shadows of his past. It was about stepping forward, accepting risk, and choosing a path of growth despite the uncertainty.

Taking a deep, steadying breath, Corin knelt once more, deliberately placing the card upon the cracked earth at the riverbank. With a decisive motion, he pressed his palm against its glowing surface, committing himself to the choice ahead.

The land shuddered beneath him, marking the moment the decision became irrevocable.

Then the ground beneath Corin trembled violently, cracks spreading outward in luminous veins of light. The river surged upward in a powerful wave, splitting dramatically into countless smaller streams that spread rapidly across the barren plains. Corin watched in awe as the earth eagerly absorbed the rushing waters.

Almost instantly, life erupted from the once-broken ground. Trees burst forth, rising swiftly with branches unfolding toward the sky, leaves and blossoms spilling outward in vivid bursts of green. Grass and flowers painted the formerly desolate landscape with vibrant colors. Corin's heart lifted with hope until movement from the river caught his attention once more.

The shadows he had glimpsed earlier now emerged fully, taking shape as serpentine forms with sleek, glistening bodies. Their eyes burned like smoldering embers, and teeth glinted sharply, dark as polished obsidian. The creatures slithered silently onto the banks, their movements graceful yet unmistakably menacing.

The voice of the Library returned, its calm tone edged with a solemn warning:

"You have awakened life, Corin, but all life carries risk. Face what you have stirred, or let it consume you."

Corin stepped back, dread pooling in his chest. The creatures advanced steadily, their dark forms twisting and coiling as they closed in, clearly intent on him.

Corin stumbled backward, his heart hammering as the shadow creatures advanced. Their movements were fluid, disturbingly graceful, their bodies slick with river water and swirling darkness. Eyes burning with sinister intelligence fixed hungrily upon him, mouths gaping to reveal jagged obsidian teeth.

Panicked, Corin grabbed a fallen branch nearby, gripping it tightly like a makeshift staff. The nearest creature lunged with terrifying speed. Instinctively, he swung the branch with all his strength but to his horror, it passed through the creature as though it were smoke, the dark form dissipating momentarily before re-forming instantly behind him.

He spun, stumbling on the uneven ground, desperately aware of how defenseless he truly was. His breath came in shallow gasps, fear clawing at his throat. The card in his palm pulsed frantically, drawing his attention downward as its symbols shifted once more, demanding action.

Corin dropped to his knees again, driven by instinct rather than conscious choice. Pressing the card firmly to the ground, he closed his eyes and silently pleaded for whatever power it held to save him from the shadows that surged relentlessly forward.

The moment Corin pressed the card to the ground, its symbols flared brilliantly, bathing him and the surrounding area in blinding light. A shockwave rippled outward, pushing back the advancing shadows. The serpentine creatures recoiled sharply, their sinister hissing rising into shrieks as the radiant barrier expanded.

He watched in awe as the circle of light continued spreading, driving the shadows relentlessly toward the riverbank. Each creature dissolved into a misty vapor upon contact with the glowing boundary, fading helplessly back into the turbulent waters from which they had emerged.

Gradually, the trembling beneath him subsided, replaced by a profound calm. The chaotic roar of the river quieted to a gentle, steady flow, its waters becoming clear and serene. As Corin lifted his hand from the now-dim card, he saw the land before him thriving, filled with new life yet bearing no trace of the darkness that had nearly consumed him.

He exhaled slowly, relief washing over him even as he felt the lingering tension. Though the shadows were gone, their echoes remained etched into his memory... warnings of the price he might yet pay for the life he had awakened.

Corin sank slowly to his knees, exhaustion and relief blending together as he gazed upon the transformed landscape. The barren, cracked earth was now vibrant with life, fields of lush grass swaying gently in the breeze, and trees spreading their branches wide toward a brilliant sky. The river flowed calmly, clear and soothing, its earlier chaos now distant and surreal.

Yet, beneath this newfound peace, Corin could still sense the shadows, faint echoes lingering at the edges of his awareness. They reminded him that even the brightest renewal carried hidden costs, consequences waiting just below the surface.

The voice returned, tinged with solemn wisdom:

"You have shaped the river and faced the shadows stirred by your choice. Life now flourishes, but remember, growth always carries risk. The brightest light casts the darkest shadow."

The card in Corin's hand pulsed once more, its glow fading as it rose gently from his palm, merging seamlessly into the shifting map upon the pedestal, now solid and tangible again. He watched, breath held, as the river's path etched itself clearly into the illuminated surface.

The chamber around him began to re-form slowly, shelves and walls materializing from the air itself. Before him, from the pedestal's surface, a new fragment of the map emerged. A clear invitation to the next challenge.

Corin stood slowly, drawing strength from the quiet resolve that had taken root within him. He knew the trials ahead would test him again, but now he felt ready... stronger for having faced the shadows within himself, and ready to step forward.

Chapter Three

THE SECOND CHALLENGE

The Mountain

The world around Corin blurred, colors bleeding into a pale haze as the final echoes of rushing water and verdant whispers faded. The vivid greens of the river's rebirth dimmed into ghostly silhouettes, until even the air felt hollow. There was no scent of moss, no warmth of sun, just cold mist and the gut-deep tug of transition.

He shut his eyes as the familiar pull of the Library gripped him once more—inexorable, like the turning of a page he could not stop from flipping.

When he opened them, he stood once more in the circular chamber.

The air here was dense and still, as though holding its breath. The light was dim but layered, spilling down from an unseen dome high above and casting fractured shadows across the carved stone floor. The pedestal at the center thrummed faintly, veins of silver and violet coursing through its sides like the lifeblood of the Library itself.

Corin staggered forward, the ache in his legs making each step a quiet protest. His clothes clung damply to his skin, still soaked with river spray from a place that no longer existed.

The map embedded in the pedestal had changed.

Where once there had been only blank stone, the river now etched its path in brilliant relief, flowing lines of light that shimmered like liquid crystal. Corin reached out, fingers brushing the river's glowing trail. It pulsed softly beneath his touch, warm and alive, as though acknowledging him.

For the first time since his arrival, a breath of satisfaction escaped his lips. The barren land had been healed. Life restored, waters flowing. It had cost him—physically, emotionally—but it was worth it.

Then the map stirred.

Its surface rippled like a disturbed pond. From the depths, another fragment emerged... a jagged shard of dark stone levitating above the pedestal. Unlike the river's smooth elegance, this one gleamed like obsidian and caught the light with sharp, menacing edges.

Corin tensed. The air shifted. The chamber grew colder.

The card in his hand pulsed once more, its warmth threading up his arm like a silent heartbeat.

"You are not finished, Corin," came the voice... deep, ethereal, without source. ***"Step forward and face what lies ahead."***

He didn't reply. Words felt small in this place. Instead, he drew in a long breath and reached toward the fragment.

The moment his fingers touched the jagged fragment, the world cracked apart like glass struck by a hammer.

The chamber vanished, its light swallowed in an instant. Wind slammed into Corin's face, sharp and sudden, stealing the breath from his lungs. He staggered, boots skidding on loose gravel, and looked up.

A mountain loomed before him.

Not a hill, not a peak but a vast wall of earth and stone, its base rooted deep in the world and its summit lost to the clouds. Its cliffs jutted upward in cruel, angular ridges, defying the sky. The air here was thinner, colder. The wind didn't whistle... it howled, a mournful, hungry sound that slid beneath his skin and clung to his bones.

Mist lingered to the upper slopes like an ancient veil, but even that could not hide the sheer scale of the mountain's defiance. Snow dusted the upper ridges, while shadows pooled in every crevice below, hiding depths that seemed to shift if looked at too long. Every breath Corin took felt like inhaling knives—thin, sharp, and bitter.

The ground beneath his feet vibrated, not with life, but with resistance. The mountain groaned deep and low, as though it were breathing or warning him.

No humming magic of the Library here. No sense of ancient knowledge or quiet guidance. This place was raw. Unwelcoming. Wild.

And alive.

From above, the voice returned. It wasn't loud, but carried on the very air itself. It was not a suggestion. It was a decree.

"The mountain stands as a barrier, Corin. It separates, shelters, and isolates. You must decide: will you carve a path through it, opening the way for others... or leave it untouched, preserving its solitude?"

Corin swallowed hard. The choice already felt heavier than the stone before him.

His eyes climbed the mountain's face, tracing its jagged ridges and sheer cliffs as if trying to find a handhold for his thoughts. It stretched so impossibly high, its slopes riddled with fractures and scars, like a monument carved by the world's own pain. A monument that had chosen to endure, unmoved.

He stood motionless for a long moment, the silence between wind gusts pressing in like a question he hadn't yet dared to answer.

To carve a path through this?

To split it open so that others could follow?

The idea felt like desecration. This mountain had stood for centuries, perhaps longer. It had outlasted empires, watched seasons cycle like breath. To alter it would be to leave a scar. A necessary one, perhaps. But a scar all the same.

And yet...

To leave it untouched meant leaving the lands on either side cut off, isolated by nature's spine. How many had turned away at its base, forced to wander far from their goals, or abandon the journey altogether?

He walked a few steps forward, boots crunching against frost-laced stone, and dropped to one knee. Slowly, deliberately, he pressed his palm to the mountain's base.

The rock was cold. Not just cold in temperature, but in memory. There was no welcome here. No invitation.

But there was potential. He closed his eyes. To carve a path meant destruction. To do nothing meant neglect. Both were a kind of violence.

A flicker of movement caught his eye. A bird, dark and small, darting from one ridge to another, wings barely visible in the mist. It flew effortlessly over what he could not climb. Free. Unburdened.

The thought ached.

"I could leave it as it is," Corin murmured, voice barely carried over the wind. "Let the mountain remain whole. Proud. Alone."

But then... it would remain just that. Alone.

As Corin crouched at the mountain's base, the cold against his palm stirred a memory—unbidden and sharp.

Snow.

Stone.

A distant cry.

He was younger then. Bolder. A leader of twenty hardened men and women, each with packs heavy with gear and hope. They had set out to cross a mountain range not unlike this one, driven by ambition and the promise of a new trade route. The maps were vague, the locals cautious, but Corin had been resolute. He remembered how he'd rallied them, how he'd spoken with confidence he didn't fully own.

"Trust me," he had said. "We'll make it."

The first few days had gone well. The weather held, the terrain challenging but navigable. Spirits were high. Jokes passed easily around fire pits. Even the wind had seemed to favor them. Until it didn't.

He saw it again now... the narrow pass they had chosen, the walls of rock rising on either side like clenched fists. He had known it was risky. The slope above had been unstable, the snow heavy with warning. But they were behind schedule. Supplies were thinning. Doubt had started to whisper among the group.

So Corin had pushed. And the mountain had answered.

The roar of the avalanche still echoed in his bones. A wall of ice and stone thundered down upon them, burying everything in a blinding white fury. He remembered the shriek of wind, the splinter of trees, the dull thud of bodies swallowed by snow.

Three lives, lost in seconds.

He saw their faces even now... Jorah, with the crooked grin. Mira, who sang to herself while packing. Halden, who always carried the map even though it was Corin who led.

Gone.

And he had brought them there.

Corin's hand trembled as he pulled it away from the stone, fingers curling into a fist. He could still see the final slope they never reached. The silence that followed. The hollow victory of survival.

The mountain before him now felt like an echo of that one.

"What if I make the same mistake?" he whispered, his voice frayed by guilt and wind. "What if carving this path... just leads to more ruin?"

The silence offered no comfort. Only the sound of wind scraping against stone, like a blade being slowly drawn.

The wind stilled.

Just for a moment. Long enough for the world to hold its breath.

Then the ground beneath Corin's feet trembled, subtly at first, like something vast shifting far below the surface. The stone responded to his doubt, not with anger, but with attention. As though the mountain had heard his whisper and chosen to answer.

The card in his hand grew warm, hotter than before. Its surface shimmered with light, and the symbols engraved upon it began to move. They twisted and bled into new forms, re-forming into two distinct images, glowing with opposing hues.

In one, the mountain stood untouched. Its cliffs were jagged and proud, its peaks crowned with snow. A monument of silence, unbroken by human hands. It exuded permanence, a symbol of endurance and solitude. A place that belonged to itself.

In the other, a narrow pass had been cut through the mountain's heart. The path was rough, uneven, carved with pain but open. And through it, light spilled. The lands beyond were visible now, not fully revealed, but no longer strangers. The divide had been crossed. Unity won through sacrifice.

Corin stared at them, heart thudding against his ribs. He didn't need the voice to explain. He understood what he was being shown.

One choice preserved the mountain but left the world divided. The other forged connection but left a scar.

The voice returned, gentler now. Not a command, but a question wrapped in gravity.

"Every choice leaves a mark, Corin. The mountain will not yield easily. Will you press forward... or let it stand as it is?"

He looked up once more at the towering mass of stone before him. It stood defiant, unbending. But beneath that, he sensed something else.

It wasn't just stone. It was memory. It was resistance. It was waiting to be understood.

He closed his eyes, the warmth of the card anchoring him.

And he chose.

Corin inhaled deeply, letting the cold fill his lungs like iron. The vision on the card still burned behind his eyes—the scarred path, the light breaking through. He gripped the fragment tighter and stepped forward.

The mountain did not welcome him.

The first incline was steep, littered with loose stones that shifted underfoot with treacherous glee. His boots scraped for purchase, the sound swallowed by the wind's rising howl. Every breath felt like inhaling glass—thin, brittle, painful.

Mist coiled along the ground in ghostly tendrils, obscuring the terrain ahead. The slope climbed without end, as if the peak existed only in theory, a concept the mountain teased but never delivered.

Corin pressed on.

The cold grew sharper with each step, no longer merely unpleasant but punishing. It gnawed at his fingers, seeped through the seams of his cloak, and sank into his bones. The card in his hand was his only warmth, its glow steady like a heartbeat but it did nothing to dull the mountain's fury.

Halfway up, the terrain turned brutal. Jagged rocks jutted from the slope like broken teeth. A ledge gave way under his weight, and he slammed against the stone, his shoulder taking the brunt of it. Pain flared white-hot. He grit his teeth, rolled over, and kept moving.

The mountain began to fight back.

The wind wasn't just cold now, it was violent. It screamed down the cliffs like a living thing, flinging grit and ice into his eyes. Shadows moved in the mist, large and slow, like the memory of giants.

The ground trembled beneath him. Not constantly, but in bursts—a warning, a pulse. Far above, cliffs groaned. A cascade of stones broke loose, thundering down in an avalanche of noise and threat. Corin barely had time to dive to the side, pressing himself against the rock face as the debris tumbled past in a storm of dust and fury.

His heart hammered. His breath came in ragged gasps. His hands were scraped and bleeding. Still, he climbed.

"This isn't just stone," he muttered between clenched teeth. "It's alive."

And it didn't want to be changed.

Higher now. The world below was lost in mist. There was only stone, wind, and the sharp rhythm of Corin's breath.

Then came the whispers.

They rode the wind, at first barely audible... half-thoughts, half-memories. But they grew louder as he climbed, threading through the air like spectral voices brushing his ears from all directions.

"Why must you break me?"

"I have stood for centuries. I held back flood and fire. I sheltered. I stood."

"You come with blade and burden. You come to cut."

Corin stopped. The wind swirled around him in tight, bitter spirals. The air thickened, the sky darkened with presence.

The voices changed, becoming more intimate. Familiar.

"Three lives lost... and for what?"

"You swore you'd never make that mistake again."

"Is this pride? Or penance?"

He turned, but there was nothing. No figure. No ghost. Only shifting fog and endless stone.

But the voices knew him.

They carried the weight of truth, echoing his deepest fears with terrible precision.

He dropped to one knee, planting a bleeding hand against the mountainside for support. The chill of it bled through him.

"I don't want to break you," he whispered hoarsely, throat raw from cold and guilt. "But some walls..."

His voice faltered, choked by wind and memory.

"...some walls need to fall."

The wind paused, as if considering. Then the card in his hand pulsed. It was not warm this time, but hot. Urgent. Its glyphs twisted again, glowing white-gold with silent command.

Corin rose, driven by something deeper than defiance.

The voices fell quiet.

The mountain was listening.

Corin stared at the mountainside before him, breath billowing like smoke in the frozen air. The silence was thicker now... expectant. No wind. No whispers. Only the weight of what he was about to do.

He drew the card from his chest with both hands. It glowed fiercely now, the warmth almost unbearable against his skin. Its sigil—ever-shifting—had stilled into a radiant glyph, etched in lines that pulsed like a heartbeat.

He stepped forward until he was nearly pressed against the wall of stone.

Then, he placed the card against the cliff face.

The mountain screamed.

A deafening crack split the silence, followed by a deep, primal rumble that shook the very world beneath his feet. Corin stumbled backward, shielding his eyes as light burst from the glyph, flooding outward in a radiant arc. The stone resisted. It splintered, groaned, fought against the power being forced into it.

And then it began to break.

The cliff face split down the center with a roar like thunder peeling across the heavens. Stone shattered outward, with purpose, cleaved by will. A fissure widened slowly, parting like ancient gates forced ajar after centuries of silence.

Corin watched as the light of the Library—soft, golden, other-worldly—poured through from the other side, casting long shadows across the broken path.

The mountain shook in protest. Dust rose like smoke. Chunks of rock fell around him, and still he stood, the card pressed against the stone until the last tremor passed.

When the dust settled, a narrow path stretched before him. Its walls were rough and jagged, lined with the raw edges of stone that bore the scars of resistance. It wasn't perfect. It wasn't smooth.

But it was open.

And through it, he saw the faint outline of trees swaying on the far slope. A new horizon. A possibility made real.

Corin lowered the card. Its light dimmed to a faint ember.

The mountain had been changed.

Its proud cliffs now bore the mark of choice. Of trespass. Of connection.

He turned and looked back with solemnity. He had carved a path but at a cost.

Corin stood at the threshold of the newly carved path, shoulders slumped beneath the weight of exhaustion. Dust clung to his cloak. Blood smeared one hand. The card in his grip had gone cool, its glow no more than a faint pulse, like the last breath of a dying star.

The mountain was silent again.

He turned slowly to take in the fissure behind him. It stretched the length of the ascent, a jagged wound cleaved through ancient stone. It was raw. Imperfect. But it was there. The divide had been breached. The way had been made.

Across the chasm, beyond the light spilling through the cut, he could just make out movement. Leaves trembled on distant trees, a breeze stirring grass on the far slope. The two halves of the world, once separated by indifference and stone, were now touching.

He had connected them.

And in doing so, broken something that had stood untouched for an age.

The voice returned, quiet this time, laced with finality. No grandeur. No riddles.

"You have carved a way forward, Corin. The mountain will stand... but it will never be the same. Progress comes with sacrifice. Remember this."

Corin said nothing.

There was nothing to say.

The wind returned, softer now... almost respectful. It carried no voices, only the sound of change. The fissure behind him seemed to breathe. Not as a wound, but as a scar beginning to heal.

The world began to fade again.

Light turned to mist. Edges blurred. The path dissolved into nothingness.

Corin closed his eyes.

And when he opened them, he stood once more within the Library.

The chamber greeted him with stillness.

No wind. No voices. Only the soft hum of ancient magic, pulsing from the pedestal like a heartbeat made of light and time.

Corin staggered forward, his legs heavy with fatigue. The echoes of stone and wind still clung to his skin, as if the mountain had left a part of itself behind in him. Or perhaps it had taken something from him in return.

The map had changed again.

Where once the mountain stood as an unbroken mass of shadow and elevation, there was now a narrow line. A glowing fracture etched through its center. The path he had carved. The scar he had chosen.

It shimmered faintly beside the flowing river, the two fragments now joined by purpose. The map was no longer a mystery. It was a memory. A testament.

And then... another fragment stirred.

From the center of the pedestal, a new shard began to rise—slowly, deliberately. This one was unlike the others. It flickered as it emerged, its surface refracting light in colors that had no name. Its edges shimmered as though dipped in smoke, refusing to settle into any fixed shape.

It pulsed with anticipation.

Corin took a step back. His fingers curled instinctively around the card, still faintly warm in his grasp.

This next fragment... felt different.

He didn't know what challenge it held, only that it would not be easier. The Library had tested his resolve, his guilt, his capacity to destroy in order to build.

What would it test next?

The chamber held its breath.

So did he.

CHAPTER FOUR

THE THIRD CHALLENGE

THE CITY

The echoes of the mountain still clung to Corin like mist. Sharp-edged memories that refused to settle. He stumbled as the chamber reassembled around him, its shifting walls forming from threads of light and shadow, solidifying into familiar stone once more. The jagged fissure he had carved into the map still glowed faintly, a scar etched into its surface, pulsing with residual power.

His legs buckled. He caught himself on the pedestal, fingers digging into the cold stone as if to anchor himself to reality. His chest rose and fell with labored breaths. The climb, the solitude, the confrontation with his own limits... it had drained him. Not just of strength, but something deeper, something unnamed.

He stared at the map, its surface no longer still. Another fragment stirred. A shard of light emerging from the center, its form wavering like a flame caught in a storm. It pulsed with erratic energy, its edges shifting between defined and formless, as if unsure of what it was meant to become.

Corin's throat tightened. He had endured the crushing silence of the mountain. He had stood against the force of the river. What challenge could remain that required such instability to herald it?

The fragment hovered just above the surface, vibrating with a warmth that reached his palm. It wasn't just heat. It was insistence. Summoning. Demanding.

He swallowed hard and reached for it, hesitating just before contact. "Let it be something I can survive," he whispered.

His fingers brushed the edge of the fragment.

The chamber fell away.

The world re-formed around him with a breathless silence.

Corin found himself standing at the threshold of a dead city. Time had not merely passed here. It had triumphed. Walls that had once towered in defiance now lay in crumbling heaps, their stones jagged and sun-bleached, half-swallowed by earth and creeping vines. The wind stirred faintly, carrying the scent of damp stone and something older—moss, mildew... memory.

He took a cautious step forward. The sound of his boots against the cracked road echoed unnaturally, warped by the emptiness. It bounced back to him twisted, as if the city resented the intrusion. He slowed, every movement deliberate, wary of the weight of the silence pressing against him.

Yet amid the ruin, beauty clung like ivy.

In the heart of a broad plaza, faded mosaics still clung to broken stone. Their colors had dulled, but their intent endured. Scenes of festivals and music, of dancers twirling beneath garlands, of laughter etched in ceramic smiles. A civilization had lived here, thrived here. Loved here.

Columns lined the walkway beyond, some shattered into chunks, others defiantly upright, their marble surfaces carved with spiraling motifs—stars, waves, branches interwoven like the dreams of those who built them.

And now... nothing.

No birds. No insects. No signs of animal or human life. Only the quiet reclamation of nature and time.

Corin tightened his grip on the glowing card in his hand, its warmth a quiet reassurance. He scanned the ruins, alert for movement, though part of him hoped none would come. There was a wrongness to the silence, as though the city itself were holding its breath, waiting.

Then the voice returned, low and measured, as if it too stood among the ruins with him.

"This was once a place of light and life, a beacon of community. Now, it is an empty monument to what was. Corin, you must decide: will you rebuild, inviting life to return, or leave it as it is, a testament to its history?"[1]

The question echoed through the plaza, and in its wake, the silence returned, heavier than before.

Corin stood unmoving in the center of the plaza, the question echoing in his chest long after the voice had faded. Rebuild... or preserve. Restore life, with all its chaos and noise and struggle—or let the past rest undisturbed, sealed in silence.

He turned slowly, taking in the remnants of the city again with fresh eyes.

Here, beauty had not merely faded... it had fractured. There was grief in the way the vines curled through archways, how the rain had eroded the artistry from the stone. But there was dignity, too. A kind of peace in the stillness. To disturb it felt almost like desecration.

He glanced down at the card in his hand. Its edges glowed more steadily now, casting a soft amber light across his fingers. It didn't push him forward. It didn't pull him back. It simply waited, ready to reflect his decision, whatever that might be.

"To rebuild is to honor their lives," he said softly, as if speaking to the air. "To leave it as it is... is to remember them."

But neither path offered certainty.

He took a step toward a fallen column, its surface cracked and worn. He ran his hand along the edge, feeling the smooth dips where countless hands had once passed. His thumb caught on a carved symbol, almost worn away. It looked like a sun.

How many people had looked to it and felt hope?

The weight of the voice's question pressed in again.

"You must decide."

---

1. ALT+42 = *

He closed his eyes. The silence was no longer passive. It loomed now—expectant. The city was watching, waiting to see what kind of man he was.

Corin moved deeper into the city, each footfall a quiet apology on the fractured stones. Debris lay scattered across the streets: shattered pottery, broken furniture, rusted metalwork twisted by time. Every piece whispered a fragment of a life once lived.

A broken jug lay beside the doorway of what might have been a bakery, its painted surface still bearing the faded image of a sheaf of wheat. Nearby, a child's toy, a wooden horse with one leg snapped clean off, lay in the dirt, half-buried beneath a layer of dust and leaf-fall. He knelt beside it, brushing it gently with his thumb, as if afraid it might disintegrate under his touch.

These weren't ruins. They were remnants of someone's everyday.

At the center of the plaza, the remains of a fountain drew him forward. Its wide basin had long since dried and cracked, the once-clear water gone, the pipes within rusted and broken. The statue that had once crowned it now lay toppled beside the base, its features weathered into anonymity. Corin crouched near it, running his fingers across the lower carvings still intact.

Figures danced along the stone. A circle of people with upturned faces, arms linked in joy. Their eyes, though chipped and faded, held a lightness that transcended time. He felt something catch in his throat.

"This place was alive," he murmured. "It mattered to someone."

The card pulsed in his hand—subtle, but steady. The voice returned, quieter now, as though acknowledging his grief.

"Life brings light, Corin, but it also brings conflict. To rebuild is to invite both. To leave it untouched is to preserve its silence, its peace. Both paths carry weight."

He looked up at the broken statue, then down again at the toy in the dirt.

It wasn't just about stone and mortar. It was about people. The lives that had been here... and the ones that might be again.

And then the memory struck.

A different city, vivid and alive—a bustling port with voices raised in laughter and bartering, the smell of salt on the breeze, music drifting from open doorways. He had spent weeks there, mapping its maze of streets, eating with strangers who had become friends. He had felt... at home.

But when he returned years later, it was gone.

The streets had been scorched black. The buildings were husks. No laughter remained. He'd learned from a passing merchant that the city had been razed... destroyed not out of necessity, but pride. A warning from one kingdom to another. And all those lives... all those stories... gone.

He stood, fists clenched.

"What if I rebuild this place," he said, voice trembling, "and the same thing happens? What if I bring people here... just to lose them again?"

The wind stirred through the plaza in response, rustling the vines, nudging the broken toy.

The city offered no answer.

Only silence.

A tremor passed beneath Corin's feet... subtle, like the exhale of something ancient rousing from sleep. He staggered back from the fountain, instincts sharpening. The air shifted, thickening around him. What had once been still and solemn now felt... aware.

Shadows moved at the edges of his vision.

He spun, heart hammering, but saw nothing, only the empty avenues, choked with ivy and silence. Yet the sense of being watched lingered, crawling across the back of his neck. He turned again. Another flicker—too fast, too quiet. The silhouette of a figure darting between collapsed walls. Or had it been smoke? A trick of the light?

His hand tightened around the card, its surface now burning faintly against his palm.

The voice returned, insistent.

"What you fear is the burden of life, Corin. To rebuild is to risk loss. To preserve is to accept stagnation. Neither path is free from consequence."

The shadows coalesced in the periphery... unformed, shapeless, yet heavy with meaning. Ghosts of what had been? Warnings of what could be? He couldn't tell. They did not attack. They did not speak. They simply watched.

The card flared in his hand, and suddenly its surface shifted, symbols rippling like water disturbed. Two images emerged.

In one, the city stood tall and whole once more, its streets alive with motion. People moved about—laughing, working, building. In the other, nature reclaimed it fully. The vines overtook stone, roots cracked through pillars, and animals wandered freely among the ruins. Peaceful. Quiet. Undisturbed.

"What will you choose?"

The words pressed against his mind like stone. He turned back toward the fountain, breath catching.

The dancing figures stared back at him. Frozen in joy. Frozen in time.

Corin stared down at the twin images glowing in his palm.

One offered renewal. Life returning in vibrant color, laughter echoing through clean streets, a second chance for what had been lost.

The other offered quiet. Nature's gentle reclamation, a preservation untouched by time or tragedy.

He closed his eyes.

He saw Marck, standing ankle-deep in the river's current, defiant and brave.

He saw himself climbing the mountain, breathless and aching, carving his path one foothold at a time.

He remembered the city. The joy that had lived there, and the fire that had taken it all away.

"Every choice I've made," he murmured, "has left a mark."

Not just on the map, but on him.

His gaze drifted to the fountain once more. The dancing figures still held hands, forever locked in celebration. Despite the ruin around them, their expressions remained untouched—hopeful, radiant. A monument to something worth remembering.

"I don't want to see this place fall again," he said aloud, voice low but steady. "But it deserves a second chance."

His hands no longer trembled. The decision wasn't easy. It wasn't certain. But it was his.

He stepped forward and knelt beside the fountain.

The card pulsed warmly in his grip, as if acknowledging his resolve. He pressed it gently to the stone base, resting it between two of the dancing figures.

A breath. A heartbeat.

Then the city began to stir.

The ground answered his choice with a sudden, deep tremor.

From the card, a golden light bloomed—soft at first, then radiant, searing. It bled into the stone beneath his hand, racing along the cracks in the fountain like fire through dry brush. Veins of light spread across the plaza, branching down streets and alleys, wrapping around ruined walls and shattered columns.

Stone groaned and shifted. Debris lifted into the air, spinning slowly before slotting itself back into place. Bricks mended, carvings re-formed. Wood stretched and reassembled into doors, beams, and rooftops, creaking as though sighing in relief.

The fountain bubbled, water surging from its basin in a brilliant arc, clear and cold. The toppled statue reconstructed itself piece by piece, rising to stand tall once more—its face restored, arms raised in eternal joy. Music, distant and sweet, floated on the air.

Corin rose slowly, eyes wide as the city rebuilt itself around him.

And then... people appeared.

Spectral forms moving through the streets as if they had always belonged. A merchant sweeping his stall. A child skipping across the plaza. A gardener tending vines that had once choked the walls but now blossomed with color.

They laughed. They worked. They lived.

But not all was bright.

From the corners of the city, dark shapes lingered. Silent figures that did not join the joy. They clung to alleyways and rooftops, barely visible, their forms wavering like smoke. Watching. Waiting.

Corin's breath caught. The city was alive again... but with life came risk.

The voice returned one last time, quiet and reverent.

"You have brought light to the ruins, Corin. What comes next is no longer in your hands. Life is risk, but it is also renewal. Remember this."

The golden glow began to fade, and the city softened into mist.

The mist curled around Corin's feet, thickening until it obscured the plaza, the streets, the ghostly faces. One by one, the voices faded, the laughter dissolved, and the city he had chosen to save vanished like a dream upon waking.

Stone re-formed beneath him.

The chamber returned.

Cold. Still. Familiar.

He stood alone once more, the pedestal before him. The card in his hand glowed brilliantly, then dimmed, its light flowing into the map like ink into parchment. The lines spread outward in a slow burn, tracing the city's rebirth across the surface. Streets formed. Walls rose. The fountain marked the center.

Where ruin had once sat empty, now a vibrant city stood.

Corin exhaled shakily, the weight of the choice settling onto his shoulders. Each challenge had left its imprint—not only on the map, but on him. He was no longer the man who had first stepped into the Library. He had carried rivers. Climbed mountains. Rebuilt the forgotten.

And still, it was not done.

The chamber remained silent, but the map stirred.

Another fragment began to rise.

CHAPTER FIVE

CORIN'S REFLECTIONS

WEIGHT OF HIS CHOICES

The chamber was silent, but the map before Corin pulsed with quiet life. A thousand tiny veins of light wound through its surface like threads of silver fire, each one tracing the path of a decision he had made. The fragments—once scattered, broken pieces of a forgotten world—now formed a living tapestry. They shimmered with faint hues: greens and blues for fertile lands and flowing water, crimson and gold where flame and risk had touched, and cold, sterile whites at the edges where his reach had not yet extended.

Corin stood motionless, his breath shallow. The silence was not empty. It pressed in, full of memory and meaning, as if the Library itself was watching. As if it, too, waited to see what he would make of the path he had carved.

He stepped closer, his boots scuffing softly against the polished floor. The map's light reflected in the chamber's smooth walls and danced across his face, casting him in shifting patterns of color—like a man caught halfway between creation and consequence. Each fragment was a record, a scar, a testament. Together, they told a story he wasn't sure he was ready to hear.

The river wound elegantly through the center, its banks lush and green, whispering of abundance. Yet in its depths, subtle coils of shadow stirred. A reminder of what he had disturbed. The fissure through the mountain stood like a wound across the land, jagged but purposeful. A bridge, yes, but also a rupture. And at the heart of it all, the city gleamed. Reborn from ruin, its streets traced with glowing promise... and hidden peril.

Corin's throat tightened. It was beautiful. And terrible. The weight of it pressed against his chest.

His fingers brushed the edge of the map. First the river, then the mountains, and finally the city. Warmth met his skin, faint and alive, as if the map breathed beneath his touch. These were the echoes of choices made, of burdens carried forward.

And they were waiting to be remembered.

Corin's fingers lingered over the river's path. The lines etched into the map glowed softly, winding across the land like a serpent at rest. But he knew better than to trust its stillness. The river had never been at rest.

He closed his eyes and the roar returned.

It was deafening, the memory of it. The crash of water against stone, the freezing pull of the current, the way it had clawed at him, dragged him down, as if trying to swallow not just his body, but his resolve. The river had not merely tested his strength. It had demanded his pain.

Marek.

The name rose unbidden, and with it, the image: a flash of red fabric caught in the torrent, a hand reaching... grasping and then gone. The ache was sharp, immediate, like it had only happened yesterday. Corin's jaw clenched, and he forced his eyes open.

The land along the riverbanks was vibrant now. Green and alive. Fields of promise that hadn't existed before. Life had taken root where once there had been only untamed water. That should have been enough. That should have been a sign that he'd done the right thing.

But the shadows beneath the river's surface told a different story.

He remembered them clearly. Forms like liquid smoke, serpentine and precise, eyes glowing from beneath the current. They hadn't fought him. They hadn't fled. They had watched. Waiting. As if his presence had been a signal. As if his taming of the river had unlocked something ancient. Something best left buried.

"Did I do the right thing?" His voice cracked in the stillness.

The question echoed in the chamber, unanswered.

Corin's gaze dropped to the polished floor. His reflection looked back—drawn, weary, hollow-eyed. A man with too many ghosts, and no way to bury them.

"What if the shadows return?" he whispered, quieter this time. "What if... what if I brought them back?"

The map offered no comfort. The Library did not speak. The silence stretched, a chasm where certainty should have been.

And in that silence, doubt took root again.

Corin's hand drifted from the river to the jagged line carved through the mountains. A deep, glowing fissure etched into the map like a wound that had never fully healed.

He remembered the cold first. Not the biting chill of weather, but the ancient, heavy stillness of a place that had never known footsteps. The mountain had not been welcoming. It had groaned beneath him, trembled under his weight, as though aware of his trespass.

The climb had taken everything.

He recalled the way his fingers had bled against unyielding stone, how the wind had howled like a voice trying to push him back. Even now, he could feel the mountain's resistance, not in his limbs, but in his soul. It hadn't wanted to change. It had endured centuries untouched, and he had carved through it.

Not with cruelty. But with purpose. Or so he had believed.

The map showed the path clearly now: a shining bridge uniting both sides of the land, two peoples no longer isolated by the mountain's impassable height. A triumph. A connection. A victory.

Beneath that shining path, the mountain bore a scar. A deep wound that pulsed with faint red light—resentful, unresolved.

"I forced it," Corin muttered, his voice hoarse. "I pushed when I should have asked."

His fingers hovered above the glowing fissure. A thin tremor ran through his hand, memory drawing forth the faces of those who hadn't made it. The crewmates, the scholars, the scouts. Some had fallen. Others had frozen. All had trusted him.

He had called it necessary. A cost of progress. But now, looking down, he wondered if that belief had been a shield for pride.

"The mountain was alive," he said softly, almost reverently. "And I carved through it like it was dead stone."

He thought of the toll, of the way the mountain had seemed to mourn as he split it. It hadn't just been a challenge. It had been a witness. And perhaps, in its silence, a guardian of something that was never meant to be disturbed.

The bridge stood. That much was true. But was it worth the scar?

Corin didn't know.

And that uncertainty cut deeper than the mountain ever had.

Corin's eyes fell to the heart of the map, where the fragments came together in a radiant nexus. The city.

Its streets glimmered with soft golden light, threading outward like veins from a beating heart. The walls stood tall once more—restored, whole, a far cry from the hollowed ruins he had first stumbled upon. In the glow of the chamber, it looked alive.

But Corin knew better.

He had walked those alleys, boots crunching over ash and shattered stone. He had stood where marketplaces had once thrived, now reduced to silence and soot. The memory rose unbidden—smoke choking the sky, flames licking through wooden beams, the stench of charred flesh still thick in his nostrils.

The city had not died quietly.

"They razed it to the ground. A warning, nothing more," the trader had said, voice flat with the weight of loss. Corin had carried those words like a brand.

Now he stared down at what he had rebuilt, and the question clawed at him: Had he simply recreated a target?

"What if I've only brought them back to die?" he said aloud, his voice brittle with guilt.

The map glowed in quiet defiance. No answer came. Only the image of a city reborn.

In the silence, he saw them again—the ghostly outlines that had shimmered along the streets during his final night there. A woman hanging lanterns from her shop's doorway. A child chasing a wooden hoop down the cobblestone lane. Two old men arguing over a game of stones. Shadows of the past or echoes of what might be.

They had not seemed afraid.

Corin pressed his palm to the fragment, the warmth of it surprising. This city had known ruin. But it had also known joy. And perhaps, given the chance, it could know both again.

"It deserves more than memory," he whispered. "It deserves hope."

He wasn't sure if hope would be enough. But it was something.

And for the first time in a long while, that felt like a reason to keep going.

Corin stepped back from the map, his hands trembling. The chamber's silence had thickened, like the hush before a storm, but no wind came—only the unbearable stillness of a place that knew too much.

His knees gave way beneath him.

He sank to the cold, polished floor, the breath leaving him in a slow, shuddering exhale. His hands came to rest on the edge of the map, fingertips brushing the glowing fragments—the river, the mountain, the city. Each pulsed faintly beneath his touch, alive with memory and meaning. His choices. His burdens.

His failures.

"I don't know if I've done the right things," he said, voice barely more than a whisper.

He wasn't sure who he was speaking to—the Library, the map, himself. The weight pressing on his chest made it hard to breathe. Each fragment was a step taken, a wound opened, a life altered. He hadn't chosen this path, not at first. But he had walked it. Every mile of it.

And now, with the end seemingly near, he felt no triumph. Only doubt. Only fatigue.

His thoughts spiraled. Marek's name flared like a wound, followed by the faces of those who had followed him into the mountain. The children of the port city. The traders, the builders, the families who had dared to hope. Every choice he had made to build something... had also destroyed something else.

Victory and mistake. Two sides of the same coin.

The Library remained silent. But it didn't feel cold. Its quiet presence felt almost... watchful. Not judging. Simply there.

Bearing witness.

Corin bowed his head, fingers curling against the stone. He had tried so hard to be strong. To be right. But in this moment, he allowed himself the truth: he was tired. Tired of choosing. Tired of carrying the cost.

His eyes fell to the card in his palm. It pulsed faintly, a soft heartbeat against his skin. The symbols etched into its surface shimmered, shifting... forming the outline of a final fragment.

Something stirred in him then. Not resolve, not yet. But the memory of it. A flicker.

He rose slowly, legs shaking beneath him, the chamber swimming for a moment before settling.

The final trial awaited.

And though doubt still clung to him like a second skin, Corin knew this: the only way forward was through.

The map shimmered beneath Corin's feet, its light growing brighter, threads of gold and silver coiling toward the center like rivers converging on a singular point. The chamber trembled—barely perceptible at first, like the exhale of something ancient stirring beneath the stone.

The final fragment rose.

It emerged slowly from the heart of the map, hovering inches above the surface. Larger than the others. Brighter. Its edges burned with a clean, white radiance—unforgiving and absolute. It cast no shadow.

The air changed.

Gone was the warmth that had pulsed from the river, the mountain, and the city. This light was colder, not in temperature but in clarity. It stripped away comfort. It demanded honesty.

Corin's breath caught in his throat. His hand tightened around the card, which now pulsed in perfect rhythm with the glowing shard. The map had brought him here, every piece of it forged by choice and consequence. But this... this was something else entirely.

The voice returned. Measured. Still.

"This is the final piece, Corin. Not a fragment of the land... but of yourself. You must shape not what lies before you, but what lies within. What you carry must be seen. Only then can the path forward reveal itself."

Corin stared at the hovering shard. There was no fear now, only a sense of gravity, like standing on the edge of something he could never undo. He reached for it.

The instant his fingers brushed its surface, the world vanished.

Light swallowed everything.

His body, the map, the chamber—gone.

He felt weightless. Exposed. Not falling, not floating—just suspended in an endless moment where the only thing that remained was him.

Silence. Breath. Corin opened his eyes.

He stood in a void unlike anything he had ever encountered—not darkness, not light, but a pale, muted nothingness that stretched in every direction. The space had no ceiling, no floor, no horizon. And yet he stood, as if the void itself cradled him. There was no wind, no sound, only the low, nearly imperceptible thrum of existence pressing around him like a heartbeat buried beneath a glacier.

He turned slowly. Nothing moved. Nothing changed.

Except for one thing.

Suspended in the space before him stood a mirror.

It was tall and narrow, framed in a dark, polished wood so rich it shimmered with an almost liquid sheen. The carvings along its edge twisted and wove together in patterns that made his eyes ache if he stared too long—familiar symbols wrapped in unfamiliar shapes. The glass itself rippled faintly, as if it were made of water, its surface pulsing with a gentle glow.

Corin felt the pull of it. Internal like a thread tied to his ribs had begun drawing him closer.

Then the voice echoed again, not aloud, but within.

"This is the Mirror of Truth. It reflects what you are... what you were... and what you could become. To know yourself fully is the final test. Only through understanding may you move forward."

Corin's mouth went dry.

He had faced ancient rivers and mournful mountains, cities lost to ruin and memory. This was different. There was no terrain to map here. No ruin to rebuild. The challenge was not of the land.

It was of the soul. His soul.

The air was thick with expectation. The void pressed inward, not threatening, but certain. This was a place where no lie could survive... not to the world, and not to oneself.

Corin stepped forward, heart pounding.

The mirror awaited.

He took another step toward it.

The ripples in its surface stilled.

Then, slowly, an image began to form. Dim at first, as though viewed through fogged glass, then sharpening with unnerving clarity.

He saw himself, years younger. Standing on the deck of a ship, hair wind-tossed and eyes lit with fire. The sea stretched behind him, endless and full of promise. Tucked beneath his arm were freshly inked maps—bold, detailed, ambitious. His expression was one of hope. Of certainty. A man who believed he could tame the unknown.

Corin felt a pang. He remembered that moment.

The image shifted... now his first major expedition. He crouched beside a rocky outcrop, sketching the contours of a coastline with steady hands. Around him, his team moved with practiced confidence. They laughed, shouted over the wind, pointed at distant landmarks. Their trust in him was implicit, woven into every movement. Corin—leader, cartographer, dreamer.

Then the sky in the reflection darkened.

The river.

The scene changed with cruel swiftness, dragging him back to that day. Rain slashed from above. The current was wild, angry. Corin stood frozen on the bank, shouting Marek's name as a flash of red cloak vanished beneath the churning water. One hand, outstretched... reaching...

Then it was gone.

Corin's breath hitched. His fists clenched at his sides.

Whispers crept into the void, curling around his ears like smoke.

"You were too proud."
"You ignored the signs."
"He trusted you."

Corin shook his head. "I didn't mean for it to happen," he whispered. "I thought I was doing the right thing."

The mirror showed him afterward. Alone in his tent, maps scattered, hands stained with ink and indecision. His shoulders slumped. His gaze hollow.

"You let the guilt consume you."
"You stopped trusting yourself."

Corin pressed a palm to the mirror, but it remained cool and unmoved. The younger version of himself faded away, leaving only his reflection—drawn, worn, and filled with old regrets.

He had chased greatness. But he had never stopped running from that moment.

Not until now.

The mirror's surface rippled again, the past dissolving into silvery waves.

When it stilled, Corin saw himself—not as a memory, but as he was now.

Older. Wearier. His face lined with exhaustion, not age. His shoulders bore the invisible weight of too many choices, too many losses. He stood in the Library, just as he had before stepping into the trial. One hand clutching the glowing card, the other resting on the map. Doubt etched into every line of his face.

This reflection didn't look back with pride or defiance.

It looked... lost.

Startlingly, the reflection spoke with his own voice, but distant, as though echoing from deep inside.

"You've carried the past for so long, it's become your compass."

Corin's breath caught.

The reflection stepped forward in perfect sync with him, mirroring every movement—yet somehow, it felt separate. Like it knew him more intimately than he wanted to be known.

"Every step you take, you question. Every choice, you second-guess. Not because you lack strength... but because you no longer trust yourself to choose."

Corin's jaw tightened. "Because I've failed before," he said aloud. "Because people died. Because Marek died."

The reflection nodded, slowly.

"And you will fail again."

Corin stiffened.

"Failure is not the enemy. It never was. The map was never meant to be perfect—it was meant to be real. To be drawn with your whole self, not just the parts you're proud of."

Corin looked down, his hands trembling. "I've spent so long trying not to make a mistake..."

"That you've forgotten how to move on."

The mirror didn't accuse. It didn't belittle.

It simply told the truth.

And that truth settled into him like a stone placed gently into water, rippling outward.

The man in the glass looked tired. But underneath the fatigue, something new glimmered behind his eyes... clarity.

The mirror shimmered once more.

Corin braced himself but this time, what emerged was not a memory, nor a wound. It was a possibility.

A man stood at the center of the image. Taller, older, but not in the way that time erodes. This version of Corin was defined by calm, not weariness. His hair had gone silver at the temples, and lines traced his face but they were not born of doubt. They were earned. Honed.

In his hands, he held a completed map—vast, intricate, filled with color and connection. It was not perfect. Some parts were smudged, others hastily drawn. But it was finished. And beautiful.

Around him stood others: travelers with packs on their backs, children with wide eyes pointing at the map, young cartographers taking notes, elders nodding with quiet approval. He moved among them with purpose, a quiet guide... respected, yes, but more importantly... trusted.

Corin stared, unable to speak.

The figure in the mirror looked up, meeting his gaze. He smiled with peace.

"This is what could be," the voice said. *"A future not defined by guilt, but by what you choose to build. You carry the past, yes. But you need not be chained to it."*

The reflection stepped aside, revealing a new map unfolding behind him—blank parchment stretched wide, unmarred, waiting.

"The path ahead is unwritten. The map is still yours to draw."

Corin's heart clenched.

He had always feared the future would mirror the past... another failure, another ruin, another name etched into memory. But this... this showed something else.

Legacy.

Not just of what he had survived.

But of what he had shaped.

And of what he could still shape, if he dared to move forward.

The image in the mirror faded, the future slipping away like mist touched by morning light. What remained was Corin's own reflection—no longer fractured by time or possibility. Just him.

Tired. Worn. But whole.

The void was still. The mirror's surface had stilled as well, returning to that silvery, liquid sheen. But there was a presence in the air now—thicker, closer. The Library's voice came again, not from the mirror, but from everywhere. Gentle. Unyielding.

"The past is a burden. The present, a challenge. The future, a choice. To leave this place, you must confront what you carry... and let go of what holds you back."

Corin's hands curled into fists.

So much of his life had been spent dragging his failures behind him like a weighted net. Every decision, every step forward, was slowed by what he hadn't done. By who he hadn't saved. And by the fear of doing it all wrong again.

"What if I can't let go?" he asked the mirror. "What if that's all I am now?"

"You are more than your grief."

The words were neither comforting nor cruel. Just true.

"What will you choose, Corin?"

The mirror offered no path. No answer. Only the question.

And it had to come from him.

He stared at his reflection, breath shallow. The man in the glass was many things—wounded, yes, but also surviving. Still standing. Still trying.

And somewhere in that truth... was strength.

Corin stepped closer to the mirror, his boots making no sound in the void.

He looked once more at the reflection—at the tired eyes, the slumped shoulders, the weight of years gathered in every silent breath. Behind that gaze was a younger man still haunted by a river, by a single outstretched hand he hadn't reached in time. A man who had built bridges and cities only to wonder if he'd damned them in the process.

But he was also the man who had kept going.

Who had dared to return.

And who now stood at the edge of something final—not the end, but the threshold of change.

His hands trembled as he lifted them, palms open toward the mirror. "I choose..." His voice cracked, and for a moment, he hesitated.

Not out of fear.

Out of honesty.

"I choose to let go of the guilt," he whispered. "I can't change what happened. But I can't keep living inside it either."

His chest tightened—but something in him released. Like a knot drawn for too long finally loosening. Tears welled in his eyes, but they did not fall. They didn't need to.

"I won't forget," he said softly, "but I won't let it chain me anymore."

The mirror responded.

Its surface glowed, not with blinding light, but with warmth—gentle and golden, like the first breath of sunrise over untouched land. Corin reached forward, and his hand passed through it effortlessly, as if it had been waiting for him all along.

The light enveloped him.

He felt weight lift from his shoulders—not vanished, but shared, as though the Library itself now bore witness to his burden, no longer letting him carry it alone.

The void dissolved.

Light receded, and form returned.

The chamber solidified around him once more—stone, silence, and the soft, ambient hum of magic alive in the walls. Corin stood exactly where he had before... yet everything had changed.

Before him, the map was whole.

The final fragment had settled into place, its glow a soft white nestled at the center, where river, mountain, and city converged. The threads of energy that connected them pulsed as one, as if the land itself had drawn breath for the first time in ages.

Corin stepped forward. His eyes scanned the completed map, and something stirred in his chest. He didn't yet know if it was pride, relief, or something deeper. The river still shimmered with life and hidden shadow. The mountain bridge still glowed along its jagged scar. The city, nestled between them, pulsed with quiet resolve.

And now, encircling them all, was a fourth path. A mirror's curve etched in light, subtle but unmistakable. A reflection not of the land, but of the one who had shaped it.

The voice spoke one last time, quieter now. Steady.

"You have shaped the map, Corin. And it has shaped you in turn. The path ahead is yours to walk. Go forward and carry what you have learned."

Corin let out a breath he hadn't realized he was holding.

The weight he'd carried was still there but lighter. Not gone, no. It would never truly leave him. But it no longer held him captive.

His hand curled around the card. It pulsed once more, gentle now, not a command, but a reminder.

The Library did not vanish. The chamber did not fade. But Corin no longer needed them to.

He turned toward the exit, the path opening ahead of him like a trail freshly drawn across parchment. The world awaited. Not a perfect world. Not a safe one.

But one he was ready to face.
And this time, he walked forward not to escape the past...
...but to embrace the future.

Chapter Six

THE DEPARTURE

The chamber dimmed around Corin as he stepped away from the map. What light remained came from the etched lines that shimmered faintly across the stone surface, pulsing like the slowing heartbeat of some ancient, living thing. The map no longer shifted or responded to him. It was still now—fixed, final. A reflection of every choice he had made within these walls.

He stood in silence, his breath shallow, as though exhaling too deeply might disturb the fragile stillness. For the first time since he entered the Library, the weight in his chest had begun to lift, though not completely. Relief came in waves—thin, uncertain, but real.

The card in his hand cooled. Its glow had faded to a quiet ember, the last flicker of a fire long burning. It rested against his skin like a fading memory—present, but no longer urgent. Corin stared down at it, letting his fingers trace its edges. Where once shifting symbols danced in alien patterns, now there was only a smooth surface, devoid of markings. Spent.

A stillness settled over the chamber, not empty, but complete. Like the final note of a song held just long enough to echo.

Corin looked around slowly. The walls that had once reshaped themselves, the symbols that once burned with impossible light, were now inert. And yet, he didn't feel abandoned. There was a quiet acknowledgment in the air, as if the Library itself watched him, not with judgment, but acceptance.

Behind him, the map pulsed one final time. A farewell.

A soft sound stirred behind Corin like stone sighing under ancient pressure. He turned, startled, and saw it: a doorway where before there had been only a blank wall. The chamber had offered no hint of a passage, yet now the stone parted cleanly, edges traced in faint, silvery light that shimmered like starlight on still water.

Beyond the threshold, there was only shadow. Not the absence of light, but something deeper, layered, and alive. The darkness pulsed with quiet motion, like a curtain caught in a slow breath. It wasn't threatening—it waited. Patient. Expectant.

Corin's feet carried him forward, slow and cautious, until he stood just before the doorway. The line between chamber and shadow was clear—tangible, like the edge of a dream. He didn't cross it. Not yet.

His heart beat faster, and he spoke aloud before he could stop himself, his voice rough and small in the vast quiet.

"Is it done? Am I ready to leave?"

The Library answered, but the voice was no longer the commanding presence it had once been. Now it was quiet, warm, almost human in its softness.

"You are not the same as when you entered, Corin. The choices you made here are yours to carry forward. You will leave, but the journey does not end. It never does."

Corin swallowed hard. The words held no comfort, yet no menace either. They were simply true.

He glanced down at the card again, watching the faint ember of its glow flicker one final time before going out entirely. He didn't know if he felt ready, or even capable but the path had opened. The only thing left was to step forward.

Each step toward the doorway echoed in the chamber like soft chimes, delicate and deliberate. Corin's legs felt heavier with every stride, not from fatigue, but from the invisible gravity of finality. This wasn't just leaving a room. It was leaving behind everything the Library had made him confront.

He stopped just short of the threshold. The silvery light along its edges cast a faint glow against his boots. Beyond, the shifting shadow stirred again, as though it recognized him now. A presence without form, waiting without impatience.

Corin took one last glance behind him.

The chamber remained unchanged. Still. Silent. The map had gone dark, its last pulse fading like breath into stone. No farewell came. No grand signal or fanfare. Just the sense that the Library had finished with him... or perhaps, that he had finished with it.

The card in his hand gave off no warmth. It was utterly inert. He turned it over. Blank. Fulfilled. Whatever bond had existed between them was done.

He held it for a moment longer, then, on instinct, slipped it into his pocket. Something about parting with it felt wrong. Even being empty it had meaning. A reminder, perhaps. A record of who he had been and what he had chosen to become.

Drawing a breath, Corin stepped forward.

The threshold met him without resistance. There was no jolt, no blinding light, no sensation of movement. Just a shift like a page turning.

And the chamber was gone.

And just like that, he was back.

No blinding flash. No swirl of stars. No triumphant fanfare. One heartbeat ago, Corin stood in a chamber of endless consequence. The next, he stood on the worn floorboards of my shop.

The scent of old parchment and exotic incense wrapped around him immediately—sharp clove, warm cedar, a hint of something unmistakably burnt (Fizzlewick, no doubt). The amber glow returned too, cradling the shelves and corners in soft light, as if the shop had simply been waiting for him to step back through.

Corin blinked, his hand still half-lifted from whatever grand gesture he'd made at the Library's end. He looked utterly displaced, standing in the same spot where his journey had begun, yet carrying the weight of miles no one else could see.

I looked up from my journal, which I most certainly had not been using to doodle strange creatures with far too many teeth. "Ah! Back already, are we?" I said, slipping off my spectacles and squinting at him.

"Not that I expected you quite so soon—or ever, really. Most who leave the Athenaeum tend to wander a while before finding their feet again."

Corin's voice was a rough whisper. "It's over?"

I smiled at that, folding my hands atop the counter. "Over?" I repeated gently, letting the word taste itself in the air. "Oh, no, my dear boy. No, no. The Athenaeum isn't a place of endings. It's... well. Beginnings. Complicated ones. Knotted up like old string. But you've come through it, and that means something."

He stepped forward slowly, the wood creaking under his boots. Every object in the shop seemed to watch him now. Books tilted forward slightly on their shelves, baubles glimmered faintly in their glass homes, a brass telescope retracted itself as if giving him space.

"I thought I'd feel... more," Corin murmured, gaze distant. "Or less. I don't know."

"Ah," I said knowingly, tapping one finger on the counter. "That's because you've changed, but the world hasn't. Very disorienting. Bit like stepping off a ship and finding the land's still swaying."

Behind him, one of the gargoyles on the lintel gave a very unhelpful snort.

"Look at him. He's barely even scorched. Are we sure he went anywhere at all?"

"Hush, you," I said aloud, waving the complaint away. "You can sniff him later."

Corin gave me a tired, skeptical look. "It still doesn't feel real."

"No, it wouldn't," I replied, stepping out from behind the counter and walking over to the small table near the hearth. "But it is. And you are. And that's what matters now."

He followed me with that faraway expression still painted across his features. The kind of look I've seen on many a traveler. Haunted, hopeful, heavy with something they don't yet know how to name.

The shop sighed around him, wood settling like an old friend shifting on its chair. Somewhere in the back, a crash followed by a muffled apology signaled Fizzlewick's continued survival.

My gaze drifted to the inside of his coat pocket, where the outline of the card still pressed faintly against the fabric. It pulsed no longer, of course. That little bookmark had done its work, same as the others before it.

I gestured toward it with a gentle nod. "You won't be needing that anymore."

Corin's hand hovered over the pocket, fingers hesitant. He pulled the card free slowly, staring at it as though unsure whether to hold it tighter or cast it aside. Its once-glowing runes had vanished completely now, leaving behind a dull, unremarkable sliver of etched brass—innocuous as a forgotten library token.

And yet, he cradled it like it still held his fate.

"It's... empty," he said quietly.

"No," I corrected with a soft smile. "It's full. Of you. All of it was."

He looked up, brow creased, searching my expression for some further truth, but I offered none. The shop was truth enough, and it didn't always come in words.

After a pause, he placed the card on the counter, fingers lingering for a moment longer than necessary. The card made no sound as it touched the wood, just a subtle shimmer of air around it, like the faintest exhale.

I swept it away with practiced ease. The motion was small, simple. Yet the act meant more than Corin knew. I did not place it in the drawer. No, not for something like that. I slipped it into the hidden groove beneath the counter, where it would eventually drift into the archives. Or perhaps into another set of waiting hands, when the time was right.

Corin tilted his head. "What happens to it now?"

I gave him the same smile I'd given every traveler who'd ever asked that question. "It finds another. The Athenaeum doesn't choose lightly. And it doesn't keep what has fulfilled its purpose."

Behind us, the floorboards creaked with a lazy stretch. A crystal orb flickered briefly on a nearby shelf, casting prismatic light over the wall. One of the books yawned. Literally. before closing itself, and drifted back to sleep.

Corin took all of it in without so much as a blink now. Good. That meant he'd truly seen the Library and come back changed.

"Well," I said, dusting off my sleeves, "now that you're not being guided by the card, your next step is entirely your own. Exciting, isn't it? Terrifying, too, but mostly exciting."

He looked at the space where the card had been, then down at his now-empty hand. His fingers curled slowly into a fist.

And I watched him carefully, quietly, letting the silence stretch. Because the truth is, that moment right there—the letting go—is more sacred than any spell or relic in this place.

Corin lingered by the door, one hand resting against the frame as though he wasn't entirely certain he was allowed to leave. The shop didn't resist him, of course, but neither did it usher him out. It simply waited—breathing quietly, watching gently, as it always did.

The outside world called to him. I could hear it too: the faint bustle of Arden's Wake beyond the alley's bend, the clatter of cart wheels, the distant gull cry overhead. Morning had likely drifted into afternoon by now, though in here, time was more of a polite suggestion than a rule.

Corin turned, eyes searching. "Will I ever go back?"

Ah. There it was. The question they all asked eventually. Sometimes with dread. Sometimes with longing. Always with that same flicker of uncertainty.

I offered a small shrug, lips curling into something that wasn't quite a smile but wasn't a no either. "Perhaps. When the time is right. The door's always there, after all. Even when you can't see it."

He absorbed that in silence, the lines on his face softening just slightly. There was clarity there now, behind his tired eyes. It wasn't peace exactly but purpose. The kind that settles into your bones when you finally stop running from the question and start walking toward the answer.

"You said it was a beginning," he said quietly.

"I did."

"And the map... it's mine now?"

"All yours," I said with a nod. "Every inch of it. You'll see that the map you now hold has always been. The Kingdom of Dunmoh was charted... by the Master Corin."

He gave a small, thoughtful nod. Not the kind you give to someone else but the kind you give to yourself when something finally clicks into place.

He turned again toward the door. The brass handle gleamed faintly in the shop's warm light, and as his hand brushed against it, the wood beneath his palm seemed to sigh in farewell.

Before he stepped through, I offered one last bit of advice, as is my custom.

"Whatever you draw next, Corin... make it yours. Don't just trace what you think the world expects."

He looked back at me, a faint, tired smile forming on his face. The first real one I'd seen from him.

"I think I can do that," he said.

He stepped outside. The door eased shut behind him with a gentle click, and Corin was gone.

I remained for a moment, still and thoughtful behind the counter. Outside, the sounds of Arden's Wake returned—soft and distant, like the city was exhaling after holding its breath. I always find it curious, that quiet moment after someone leaves. The shop feels a little emptier, yes, but also a little more fulfilled.

Sometimes I peek, you know. Just a little.

Out beyond the brick and fog, Corin stepped back into the alleyway but it didn't greet him as he remembered. Already, the world was shifting again. The shop does not cling. It releases.

The alleyway narrowed with each step he took. Shadows stretched, edges blurred. And when he reached the mouth of the street, he turned back. Some instinct urging him to see if we were still there. All he found was a brick wall. Weathered. Cold. As though it had stood undisturbed for a century or more.

He raised his hand, pressed his fingers gently against the stone. It did not give. It did not shimmer or ripple or hum. Just old, familiar brick. Ordinary. Comforting.

Corin gave it one last pat. I could almost feel it from here. A thank-you, perhaps. Or maybe a goodbye.

He turned, shoulders a touch straighter than when he entered, and stepped out into the flow of the city. Arden's Wake swallowed him up as it does all travelers but this time, he didn't resist it. He walked with his eyes open. With his heart open.

In his hand, he clutched a pencil and a notebook, the pages still mostly blank but not for long. As he moved down the street, he opened to the first clean page and, without hesitation, began to draw.

The lines came easily now. Not perfect, no but real. Honest. Each mark a decision. Each stroke a promise. A map not of where he'd been, but where he might yet go.

And above him, the sky stretched wide. Crisp air. The scent of the sea. A new day.

I smiled.

The door behind my counter creaked as Fizzlewick emerged, a feather duster caught in his belt and two books teetering in his arms. "Did he make it?" he asked, peering around the shop.

"He did," I said, returning to my journal. "And now... he begins."

CORIN'S REACH
FROS
FOXBURROW
SNOWHAVEN
ELDERWOOD FOREST
FERNSHADE
HAV
GLADECROSS
BRIARSHADE
LOWBRANCH
MOSSWICK
V
P
OAKRIDGE
SEABREEZE
WHALESONG BAY
ANCHORSTONE
TIDEMARCH
TWILIGHT CO

Elder Mountains
Kellgrim's Rest
Eagle's Perch
Breyton
tle Dunmoh
Braeland
Pearlmoor
Arden's Wake
ANT
INS
Stonebrook
Silverport
ROOK
Stormhaven
T

EPILOGUE

The air in the alley shifted—not with wind, but with intent.

A whisper of light traced itself into being near the old brick wall where, moments before, a shop had once stood. The light deepened, spiraling upward from the cobblestones like a vine of moonlight threading through soil. It twisted with purpose, glowing brighter with each breath until a figure took shape within its heart.

Clara's feet touched the ground softly as the magic completed its weave. Her cloak fluttered gently around her boots, the lingering threads of her spell unraveling like the final lines of a fading melody. She drew in a sharp breath and exhaled slowly, eyes closed as the last word of her incantation echoed in her mind.

When she opened them, the forest was gone.

She now stood in a narrow alleyway tucked behind a row of shops in Arden's Wake—though the city's hum felt like a distant memory beneath the strange stillness here.

"Well, well..." came a voice. Low. Mischievous.

"A visitor, perhaps?" a second chimed in, skeptical and nasally.

Clara blinked, staggering a half-step as the cobblestones tilted beneath her boots. She turned sharply, scanning the shadows. There was no one. Only two small stone gargoyles perched above a faded wooden sign that read Curiosities, the letters just crooked enough to make her squint.

"Naw... not this one," the first voice said again, more certain this time. "She's not ready yet."

Clara narrowed her eyes, heart racing slightly. "Who said that?"

Silence.

She turned in place. The alley was empty. Completely so. But something about the space clung to her. It wasn't threatening, but rather watchful. Familiar in a way she couldn't explain. Her gaze returned to the shop door, where the gargoyles stared in eternal mockery.

They couldn't be real. She shook her head, reaching out to steady herself against the wall. The bricks were cool beneath her fingertips, rough and solid. The scent of the city's morning drifted in from beyond the alley—fresh bread, smoke, a hint of sea air.

Clara inhaled deeply, grounding herself. Whatever magic she had conjured, it had brought her here for a reason... though why remained elusive.

She straightened her cloak, brushed the dust from her sleeves, and moved toward the street. Her boots made no sound as she crossed the threshold from the alley to the open world.

And when she turned back...

The alley was gone.

A plain brick wall stood in its place. Weathered. Unremarkable. As though it had always been there, as though nothing magical had ever touched this place at all.

Clara stared for a long moment, brow furrowed.

"Weird..." she murmured.

Then she turned, tucked her hands into her sleeves, and melted into the crowd.

The wall behind her remained still. Watching. Waiting. And somewhere deep within the folds of elsewhere, a certain shop chuckled to itself.

9 798999 896780 1